"Ar__
going to get married."

Lisa's sudden question was surprising.

"Uh...I don't know," Jeanne answered honestly. "How do you feel about it?"

"Well, we sure need a mom!" said Lisa, frank in the way only a child can be. Then, "specially when we're sick." She kicked a rock. "Everybody in my class has a mom. Some of 'em don't have dads, but *everybody* has a mom!"

Jeanne was still thinking about this when the little girl asked, "Am I talking your ear off? Daddy told me not to."

Laughing, Jeanne assured her, "Certainly not." Then she squeezed the little girl's hand.

Lisa squeezed back. "I *like* you, Jeanne!"

Lynn Russell is a mother who works full-time, but she still manages to find time to write. She often makes up stories on trips, and while driving through the foothills of Montana, she decided to set a story in that beautiful part of the world. *Montana Christmas* is that story. It's also Lynn's first published novel.

In memory of my son Matthew

MONTANA CHRISTMAS

Lynn Russell

WORLDWIDE®

TORONTO • NEW YORK • LONDON
AMSTERDAM • PARIS • SYDNEY • HAMBURG
STOCKHOLM • ATHENS • TOKYO • MILAN
MADRID • WARSAW • BUDAPEST • AUCKLAND

Special thanks and acknowledgment to
Donna L. Scofield

ISBN 0-373-83288-5

MONTANA CHRISTMAS

One

Jeanne twisted to look over her shoulder, trying to see her back in the dresser mirror. She sighed. It had been so long since she'd even cared what her back looked like, as long as it was covered with a white uniform or a warm flannel pajama top. What if her idea of "classic casual" was this Hank person's idea of "depressed dowdy"?

Emily, her three-year-old daughter, patted Jeanne's leg reassuringly. "You look pretty, Mommy."

Jeanne smiled down at her. "Thanks, honey." She turned to face the mirror, looped her dark brown hair loosely behind her ears, then whispered frantically, "No, no, no!" Hands moist with nervousness, she pulled the barrette out and fluffed the hair with her fingertips. Her dark brown eyes sparkled with what she hoped Hank would think was fun and enthusiasm; she knew, however, the sparkle was sheer panic.

It was almost funny. The only difference between this blind date and that horrible one in high school was that this time there was no zit on her nose. *Or was there?* Phew! Just a shadow, thank heavens, because creamy skin was one of the few things about her appearance she felt satisfied with. Well, she'd never claimed to be a raving beauty, and Hank *had* seen her picture.

She stepped back from the mirror to get as full a reflection as possible. Was her tummy popping out just a bit? She inhaled deeply, turned sideways and checked the mirror. No, just her imagination. The gray flared skirt she'd finished hemming only an hour ago had flattering princess lines, and she was pleased to see that the new pink sweater added a becoming flush to her cheeks. Good thing. She'd bought it yesterday at Nordstrom's for more money than her monthly utilities bill; it had damned well better make her look good!

Jeanne stood in the archway between miniscule kitchen and tiny living room. Clean, comfortable-looking, a bit shabby—but he shouldn't expect more. Hank Gustafson knew she was a single parent, making it on her own with a little girl. Just as she knew he was a single parent, struggling to provide a home for his daughter and two sons and run a 2,000-acre ranch at the same time.

Other than both being alone, the only thing Jeanne Fremont and Hank Gustafson had in common was a woman named Paula—Hank's sister and Jeanne's new best friend—who had talked them into this meeting, certain that they would be able to make each other's life complete. The eternally optimistic matchmaker.

The buzzer from the lobby rang while Jeanne was filling the coffeepot. Her hand jerked and she spilled the paper liner full of dry coffee into the sink. The caller was Hank. She spoke into the intercom in a voice more breathless than she would have liked, then quickly spooned more coffee into the basket and still had time to open the door at the first rap, leaving the knocker's knuckles suspended in midair.

"Uh...hi!" Jeanne said softly, hoping he wouldn't notice the rapid pulse beating in her throat. Aware she was staring, she pulled her gaze away and held out her hand for a handshake. But Hank was already shrugging out of his jacket, and he laid it across her extended arm. She turned to hang his coat in the closet, breathe deeply and quiet her nerves.

Paula had described her brother's humor and kindness, his devotion to his children and the stubborn tenacity with which he clung to the family homestead, but she hadn't said a word about how handsome he was. And the snapshots she'd seen hadn't revealed how his sun-bleached hair smoothed back from a tanned forehead, nor how his deep blue eyes emphasized the planes of his craggy face. The age-whitened jeans and soft corduroy jacket came as no surprise, although she was a bit amazed that a Montana rancher shared the fashion sense of Tom Cruise. But she definitely wasn't prepared for the way her heart sped up when she tipped her head back to look up into his face, or for the surprising way his warm smile seemed to light up the whole room. Good Lord, she thought, so the three kids had driven his wife crazy and the ranch was isolated and she yearned for fun and excitement, but how on earth could she have run off and left him?

Emily broke the awkward silence. Tugging at her mother's skirt, she exclaimed wonderingly, "Mommy, look, he's wearing cowboy boots!"

Hank looked down at his toes as if surprised. "I'll be darned!" he said. "So *that's* what was making so much noise out on the sidewalk!" He bent down to

Emily's level. "I'm sorry, ma'am. Next time I'll wear my Sunday best."

Emily gave him a serious, brown-eyed gaze. "That's okay. I like cowboy boots."

Bringing coffee and cookies from the kitchen, Jeanne was glad she'd insisted on this private first meeting, even though, right now, it seemed somewhat stilted and awkward. Paula had wanted a big family dinner at her place: Hank and his three kids, Jeanne and Emily, and of course Paula and Al and their two. It would be so much more relaxed and casual, she had urged. But Jeanne had stood fast. She'd see how Emily liked him and how she herself liked him, and take it from there. So calm, cool and collected she had been back then, arranging this meeting. Who would have dreamed that his grin would turn her to jelly?

Jeanne offered the plate of cookies to him. "What do you take in your coffee?" she asked. "Careful, Em, that milk glass is pretty full."

"Just black." He took a bite. "Great cookie."

"Chocolate never fails." The instant the words were out Jeanne wished them back. Which was worse? she thought. Sounded as if she was trying to be Little Miss Homemaker or doing a study on the cookie preferences of the blind date. She hoped that writhing on the inside didn't show on the outside.

Hank chewed a moment, eyes following Jeanne as she poured herself a cup and sat down. "This has got to be the most awkward first date in the world." His voice was rueful.

Jeanne took a cookie herself. "Still, maybe it's better. We don't have to mess around with 'What do you do?' and 'What do *you* do?' and 'What's your sign?'"

Hank chuckled and sipped his coffee. "I see you've done the singles bit."

"Actually, no." No feigned sophistication. That's what she'd decided when finally agreeing to go along with Paula's matchmaking. She knew that honesty had to be not just the best, but the *only* policy. "I haven't done the singles scene. I just read a lot."

He nodded. "Me, too. Up where I live, you either read a lot or go crazy. No, wait, strike that. I'm supposed to be selling you on the quiet country life." At her wary glance, he stopped. "No, we're not selling each other on anything. That's what we agreed. Complete honesty." He extended his hand to shake on it, and the moment his warm, work-hardened hand took hers, Jeanne knew, with a sinking heart, that what she was feeling was definitely not what she had planned. But she gave him a firm businesslike handshake, anyway, and sank back into her chair, hoping her hand didn't leave a charred imprint on her new skirt.

She still couldn't believe she had agreed to meet this perfect stranger—object, if all went well, matrimony. Up until three months ago she and Emily had managed just fine. She was accustomed to being alone. Her parents had died in a car accident when she was seven, and the aunt and uncle who'd raised her, although they had been scrupulously fair in handling her parents' insurance money, left no doubt they were only doing their duty. Jeanne had gone away to college with no regrets and no lingering goodbyes.

She had dated little during high school. Girls less attractive than she had steady boyfriends or played the field, but something in Jeanne's quiet reserve pinned a little Do Not Disturb sign on her slender shoulders.

At college she made a determined effort to drop the reserve, which met with some success. But it wasn't till near the end of her final year of nursing school that she fell head over heels in love with a med student who seemed to return the feeling. Jeanne threw her whole being into the relationship. When she told him she was pregnant, instead of responding with marriage plans as she'd expected, he said, "Are you sure I'm the father?" She was crushed and bitter.

Now Emily's voice brought her back to the present. "Where're his kids, Mommy?" The little girl sounded disappointed. "In the picture he had kids." She turned to Hank. "Did you leave your kids at home?" she asked reproachfully.

"No, they're at their aunt Paula's house. You know Paula, don't you?"

Emily nodded. "Can we go see them?"

"Maybe later, honey," Jeanne said.

"Can they go to the Children's Village with us?" Emily preferred to get arrangements nailed down; no dangling "maybes" for this child.

Hank's expression was serious as he turned to Emily. "Tell me what it's like, and maybe we can go tomorrow."

Emily launched into a detailed description of the Children's Village at Seattle Center. "Oh, it's wunnerful. It's got teensy houses and stores that kids can play in and pretend to be the grocery man or the library lady. It's got a big huge tower made out of Lego. Sometimes it's got science 'speriments or contests, like who can blow the biggest bubble..." The child's shyness vanished as she edged closer to Hank, caught up in her description.

Jeanne watched, amazed and relieved. Emily had always been a quiet child, and the hardship of the past three months had left her a bit wary of strangers, with a tendency to cling closely to her mother. Her quick response to Hank was reassuring. Jeanne let her chatter on for a few more minutes, then, when her travelogue began to wind down, seized the opportunity. "Time for bed, Em."

With Emily tucked in for the night, Hank's and Jeanne's conversation grew more serious. "When my sister first mentioned you," Hank began, "she said that although she hadn't known you before your accident, she'd learned from others that you'd been very self-reliant, very independent." His deep blue gaze was questioning. "That must have made being completely helpless like you were even harder."

Jeanne nodded, peering into her coffee cup. "It was horrible. When I came to, the last thing I could remember was pushing Emily toward the sidewalk. For all I knew the car had hit her, too. Even when they assured me she was okay, I was still crazy. Thank God your sister was a mother—it helped her understand how I felt. When she walked in carrying Emily I finally calmed down."

She smiled in remembrance and took a sip of coffee. Paula had been the social worker assigned to finding a temporary placement for Emily when the child and her unconscious mother were brought to the hospital. After Jeanne regained consciousness, Paula had helped Jeanne make arrangements with a friend to care for the little girl, and Emily was able to go back to the familiar day care that St. Vincent's Hospital offered its employees, staying with her mother's friend at night. It was a workable solution, but it made

Jeanne realize the awful vulnerability of Emily's situation. *She* could safeguard and protect Emily from the world, but if something happened to her, Emily would be completely alone.

Jeanne ran her finger around the rim of her cup distractedly. All the cards on the table—that was what she'd decided. "Did Paula tell you about Emily's father?"

"No. Probably didn't think it was any of my business."

Jeanne swallowed painfully. What if her next words sent him away? Or worse, made him think she was available for some free and easy fun?

"Well," she said, "if anything comes of our meeting, it is your business." She cleared her throat. "I haven't seen Emily's father since the day I told him I was pregnant. Evidently marriage didn't seem like a great idea to him." Strange how that still stung. Even though four years had dulled the original pain, knowing you'd meant less than nothing to someone you thought loved you was hard to face.

"Then he's a first-class jerk, and you're better off without him," Hank said bluntly. Then his face and voice softened. "But I know it's been hard for you. Paula told me that much."

Jeanne nodded. "I shudder to think how things might have been if Paula hadn't been assigned to me. When she took Emily and me home with her, she was definitely stepping outside her job description, but it meant I could be released weeks sooner—they hadn't been going to let me out till I was completely able to care for myself." She smiled, remembering Paula and the kindness of her studious husband and two children. Jeanne looked Hank full in the face. Might as well be perfectly frank. "Of course, it was during those weeks that she decided I was the perfect lost soul to fill your need."

"Lost soul? Ha! You've got too much going for you to be a lost soul." Hank stared into his almost empty cup. "How much did she tell you about the situation the kids and I are in?" Then he shook his head. "Never mind, don't answer that question. I'll tell you." He was silent for so long that Jeanne thought perhaps he'd changed his mind. Finally, "It wasn't so much that we were too young to get married, although that was part of it. We were in college. I was majoring in agribusiness so I could take over the home place. Cyndi was majoring in parties." He put his cup on the coffee table. "No, scratch that statement. I've got to be fair." He sat forward, gripping his hands together tightly between his knees. "It's kind of like your story, but with a different ending. She told me she was pregnant, and as far as I was concerned, marriage was the only answer. I knew she hated the ranch—one weekend there had been enough for me to see that. But I was crazy about her, and I figured she'd change. I guess... I guess I trapped her." His words came faster now, tripping over themselves.

"After Lisa was born, during that first year and a half on the ranch, Cyndi begged me to give it up and move to Helena, or better yet, Spokane. I should have listened to her. Instead, I got her pregnant again." He breathed deeply, striving for control. "That was bad enough. The third pregnancy was unbelievable. By that time we practically hated each other. But it happened."

He was silent for so long that Jeanne finally whispered, "How did it end?"

"She just left. I got one note from her, bubbling with excitement. She'd met up with some guy who was going to help her become a model. Over the next few months there were a couple of phone calls, when she'd either had too much to drink or was on drugs. After that, nothing. Then about a year ago her mother called me."

Jeanne snatched a quick glance to see if he was visibly upset, but except for clenched fists he wasn't, at least not outwardly.

"She said she was going to report Cyndi as a missing person, because she hadn't heard from her in a long time and she thought Cyndi had been taking a lot of chances."

"Like what?"

"Like drinking with strangers, and sleeping with strangers, and hitchhiking."

"Oh," Jeanne answered in a tiny voice, wishing she hadn't asked.

"I just figured Cyndi was enjoying life in the fast lane, but after the missing-persons report was filed, her mother learned she'd died in L.A. several months earlier."

"How did she die?"

"Drug overdose." Hank shook his shoulders, as if trying to rid himself of a physical burden.

"So then did your mother-in-law want to see more of the children, to sort of take Cyndi's place?"

"Nope. She'd never seen the baby, and she'd only seen the older two twice. She said, and I quote, 'It's less painful for me to just seal off the whole business as if it never happened.' And I guess she did just that. We haven't heard from her since."

"Oh, my." Jeanne was a little overwhelmed. Although Paula had told her the bare bones of the story, hearing it in Hank's tightly controlled voice brought the reality of it to her. "I'm so sorry."

Hank unclenched his fists, sat back and smoothed his hands on the thighs of his jeans. He drew a ragged breath and said, "Now, back to you. Paula's pretty intuitive, I'll admit that. She certainly knew I needed help. But you? I can't understand why you're worried about security and a family for Emily."

"What do you mean?" Jeanne sat up straighter.

"Well, even if Emily's father was a jerk and left you bitter, you're pretty enough to have found somebody else long ago. I'm amazed you're still alone."

Jeanne spoke with studied calm; this had been deeply thought through. "Most men aren't interested in a ready-made family. I don't want Emily ever to feel like she's in the way, like she's somebody's duty. I'd spend my whole life alone before I'd do that to her." Her eyes appraised him evenly. "Of course, that's why the whole bunch of us, your family and mine, are going to get well acquainted before we even think of carrying your sister's idea any further." The coolness of her voice belied the rush of delight at the very thought of Paula's goal.

After several weeks of getting to know Jeanne better than anyone ever had before, Paula had decided that she and her brother were made for each other. And now, after weeks of refusal, then doubtful consideration, then dubious halfway agreement, followed by weeks of exchanged letters, snapshots and phone calls, Paula's idea was being put to the test.

"Tell me about your children," Jeanne said, her voice warming. This was a safe subject; she could talk about the three youngsters without betraying the unexpected effect their father had on her. "I saw the pictures Paula has. They're cute kids."

Actually, it was when she saw Paula's pictures that she felt the first tug of interest in her new friend's harebrained idea. There was a wistfulness in the little girl's face, a protectiveness in the way she stood with an arm around the shoulder of each of her little brothers, that went straight to Jeanne's heart. "How old did you say they are?" she had asked Paula, noting the girl's too-short dress and too-long bangs, the jagged rip in one boy's jeans, the way a wide band of the tiniest boy's tummy was exposed between his short T-shirt and sagging pants.

"Lisa's six and a half—she's in the first grade. Timmy's five and Joey's four—they're a regular handful," Paula had responded. "I can understand their mother feeling she was in over her head, but how could anyone walk away and leave an eight-month-old baby? That's how old Joey was when she left." She shook her head. "Hank's managed on his own for over three years now. Oh, Ma helps when she can—she came and stayed with them when Cyndi first left, but her health is poor. She was forty when I was born, you know. She and Dad had long given up on having kids." Paula laughed. "Then Hank came along four years later." She flipped back a few pages in the album, to a picture of a couple, well past middle age, standing arm in arm with a pair of teenagers, a big two-storied farmhouse flanked by cottonwood trees in the background. "Daddy died not long after this picture was taken," she mused. "Ma managed as long as she could with the year-round hired man and his wife, and extra help during summer, but she was so relieved to turn the place over to Hank when he dropped out of college and brought Cyndi home. She'd been having heart problems for at least a year and hadn't even told us."

Jeanne brought herself back to the present. Hank had reached into his shirt pocket and pulled out a packet of pictures. "These are pretty recent," he said proudly. "Here's one I took of Lisa on her first day of school." Jeanne studied the snapshot he held out to her. The little girl was wearing a big grin and a colorful gingham dress. Instead of being too short, this dress was woefully long, obviously purchased with enough room to grow into. Poor little kid, Jeanne thought. Her father obviously tried his best, but didn't quite succeed. Lisa looked like a child from the nineteenth century.

"Does Lisa like school?" she asked.

Hank frowned. "Not much," he admitted. "In fact, she was thrilled when I withdrew her for a week for this trip." He glanced defensively at Jeanne. "The teacher sent books," he said quickly, "and Paula and I plan to help her with her reading."

"Maybe I can help, too," Jeanne murmured. "For years I'd wanted to be a teacher, then changed to nursing." What am I doing? she thought in amazement. I haven't even met these kids!

Two

She met them bright and early the next morning. Before going to bed the previous night, Emily had convinced her mother and Hank that a trip to the Children's Village at Seattle Center was a must, preceded by breakfast at the nearby pancake house where she and her mother ate whenever they made the trip. "Hey, maybe Paula and Al and the kids would like to come along, too," Hank suggested.

He brought his three children upstairs with him when they stopped at Jeanne's apartment to pick them up for the outing. Emily shyly disappeared behind her mother's denim-clad leg; Joey did the same with his father. Lisa and Timmy bravely stepped forward and offered their hands to Jeanne when Hank introduced them. "I'm very pleased to meet you, Mrs. Fremont," Lisa said, the phrase sounding as though her aunt Paula had finished the final rehearsal just moments before in the lobby downstairs. Timmy echoed the statement, a syllable behind his sister.

"Just call me Jeanne, like your cousins do," Jeanne murmured awkwardly. Even after four years of pretense, the "Mrs." still made her uncomfortable. She bent to their level and pulled Emily from behind her, and Hank did the same with Joey. Although the two youngest were quiet and shy for a while, Emily's experience at day care left her more outgoing with children of her own age than her mother had ever been, and by the time they arrived at the pancake house, all six kids were chattering nonstop. Paula's son and daughter, who shared friendship with both Emily and their younger cousins, were just enough older to see that all the kids felt welcome and included. As Jeanne cut Emily's pancakes into bite-size pieces and Hank did the same for Joey, Jeanne remembered the times she had envied large, happy family groups like theirs.

They had a wonderful day at the Children's Village. Although all the kids were tired and cranky by the time the outing was finished, the day still seemed to retain a certain glow. Paula's two children had good-humoredly helped shepherd the younger ones through the Center. Once during the afternoon Lisa had lagged, limping slightly, then willingly settled on a park bench while Jeanne sat beside her, searching in her bag for a bandage for the little girl's heel. "What pretty new shoes, Lisa," she said, "but they're rubbing your heel. You're going to have one heck of a blister by the time we're through."

"Daddy told me I should wear my tennis shoes, but I wanted to look nice," Lisa answered softly. "Daddy bought these new school shoes for me yesterday. My tennis shoes are old and yucky." Aha, Jeanne thought. Could we have here the reason Lisa doesn't like school? With her too-long or too-short dresses and yucky tennis shoes, have kids made fun of her?

"Are your old tennis shoes back in the van?" Jeanne asked, hoping they hadn't been thrown away at the shoe store.

"Yes, but I don't think Daddy will want to go back and get them, not after he told me and told me I'd be sorry if I wore these new shoes."

"Maybe you and I could go back together and get them," Jeanne suggested. And they did. Hank raised his eyebrows questioningly when Jeanne asked for the car keys, and she gave him an answering wink. Then she and Lisa walked slowly back to the van, Lisa carrying one shoe and sock and chattering a mile a minute about the ranch, her cat named Boo, their swaybacked old horse, Pat, the long bus ride to school. Suddenly she stopped.

"Am I talking too much?" the child asked, stricken. "Daddy told me this morning not to talk your ear off."

"You're certainly not talking my ear off!" Jeanne assured her, wishing she could give Hank Gustafson's ear a tweak for putting doubts in the mind of his daughter, who already had so little self-confidence. They continued in silence for a moment.

"Are you and my daddy going to get married?" Lisa asked suddenly.

"Uh...I don't know." Jeanne answered honestly. "How do you feel about that?"

"Well...we sure need a mom!" said Lisa, frank in the way only a child can be. Then, wistfully, "'specially when we're sick." She kicked a rock with her shod foot. "Everybody in my class has a mom. Some of 'em don't have dads, but *everybody* has a mom!" Jeanne was still thinking about this when the little girl asked her next question. "Do you have a curling iron?"

"Pardon?" Jeanne said, unable to quickly bridge the gap between "everybody has a mom" and "curling iron."

"Allison's mom uses the curling iron on Allison's hair every morning, and the teacher says, 'Oh, Allison, what beautiful curls you have!'"

Jeanne grabbed Lisa's hand and swung it in her own. "Yes, I have a curling iron, Lisa." She sneaked a look out of the corner of her eye at the child. "I kind of know how to cut hair, too. And I have a sewing machine—I love to sew stuff for little girls." A small smile was playing around the corners of Lisa's mouth. Jeanne swung their hands higher; Lisa did a little skip. "I'll bet we could make Allison turn green with envy," she said, "and shock the teacher's socks off!"

Lisa looked up at her, a twinkle in her eyes. "Do you know how to make cupcakes?"

"Sure, with fancy stuff on top, too."

"Allison says her mother's going to send clown cupcakes to school on her birthday." She kicked another rock. "Her birthday's just before Christmas."

"When's your birthday?"

"Couple weeks, right after Thanksgiving."

"Hmm. What's fancier than clowns?" mused Jeanne.

Lisa squeezed her hand, face glowing. "I *like* you, Jeanne!"

Three

The next day, Sunday, they went to the aquarium and had lunch at Ivor's Acres o' Clams. Jeanne had arranged to have Monday and Tuesday off work, although, thanks to her lost income because of the accident, she really couldn't afford to. But she did it, anyway, and they filled both days with fun.

On Monday they hit the Pike Street Market right after it opened, stopped at a muffin place for refueling, then tackled the walking tour of underground Old Seattle. They took the boat tour of Seattle harbor, treated themselves to gooey pizza for dinner, then collapsed into a row of seats for the latest Walt Disney movie. On Tuesday, it rained, but that didn't stop them. They had lunch in the Space Needle restaurant. After that, since the rain had let up a bit, they stood out on the deck in the gentle drizzle and the kids fed quarters into the telescope so they could watch the slowly revolving landscape.

"The children get along pretty well, don't they?" Hank observed, after Lisa had maturely stepped in when Timmy tried to elbow Emily away from the telescope before her turn was finished.

"Yeah," Jeanne murmured. Hank was holding the umbrella and had casually draped his other arm around Jeanne's shoulder. Just remembering to breathe was difficult; sparkling conversation was definitely out of the question. She rallied. "Of course, with four kids there'd always be a dull roar in the background."

"Oh, sure," he agreed. "And think of when they're teenagers—two prom dresses, two tuxes, four kids learning to drive."

Jeanne's head swam. They hadn't seriously discussed the future, although of course it was in the backs of their minds. After all, they had met for a purpose. Her shoulder was nestled under his arm; she could swear she felt his heart thudding away. Could she possibly hope that Hank's feelings for her were growing? How could she be such a dreamer? Although his presence turned her to mush, she was afraid that as far as he was concerned she was simply a practical solution to a problem—maybe a little more attractive solution than he had expected, but still just a solution.

So, she told herself, maybe ours won't be the great American love story. It'll have to do. And I'll learn to control my heartbeat, and I'll never be made a fool of by reaching out to someone who doesn't want me. Once burned, twice smart, or something like that. "That sounds so permanent," she said. "We haven't really talked about the future."

"Then we need to."

That evening they left all the kids with Paula and had dinner at a charming Italian restaurant. Over cocktails they discussed the obvious: the way their kids seemed to hit it off. Around bites of salad they explored the questionable: could she be happy isolated on a ranch for weeks at a time, sixteen miles from a store, thirty-five miles from the nearest one-horse town, sixty miles from Helena? And Spokane, the nearest *city,* was too far away even to talk about!

Jeanne skewered a bit of radicchio on her fork and swirled it in the vinaigrette dressing. "The isolation isn't a problem," she said. "I learned to entertain myself alone from the time I was a child." She grinned. "But, I don't really think I'll have to worry about entertaining myself with four kids and a house to take care of."

"And a husband," Hank added quietly, taking a sip of wine.

Jeanne hoped the warmth she felt in her cheeks wasn't visible. What did he mean? But she was getting better at presenting a calm front. "Well, yes, a husband," she conceded. "Are you a pipe-and-slippers guy?"

"Nah," Hank conceded, "although sometimes after a really hard day I need help pulling my boots off."

Luckily the arrival of their garlic shrimp interrupted that train of conversation.

"So, what do you say?" Hank's voice was still quiet, perhaps even tense. "Shall we join forces?"

"Goodness, I don't know if I can handle so much passion and romance," Jeanne replied lightly. "Fetch the smelling salts! Give me air!"

Hank grinned. "That *was* pretty bad, wasn't it? But it's hard to know how to do this. I mean, my sister brought us together for this purpose, but still, it's got to be more than a business deal." His hand covered hers on the snowy linen cloth. "Don't you think so?" he persisted. "Don't you think it's got to be more than just business? We're going to be raising four children together, after all.''

So that's how it is, Jeanne thought. Raising children together. Well, that's all I was counting on at the beginning. It's not his fault I seem to be falling for him. "Yes," she said calmly. "We'll need to be each other's best friends, not just business partners." She gently withdrew her hand and picked up her wineglass.

There was a heavy silence. "I...I hope we'll be more than best friends," Hank said haltingly. "After all, we're a healthy man and woman. I...I want us to be husband and wife in every sense." Her eyes widened and he said quickly, "Oh, not right away, of course. I mean, not till you're...till we're ready. I'm not some high-school kid with raging hormones."

A petty part of her was enjoying his discomfort, she realized. He blundered on. "I mean...we'll just take it slow and easy, and we'll know when the time is right."

"When the time is right—that sounds suspiciously like breeding a prize mare," Jeanne said lightly. Then at the confusion on his face, she added, "Never mind, I know what you mean."

Four

Able to get the three-day waiting period waived, they were married Thursday evening in Paula's living room by the minister of the church her family attended. A few of Jeanne's coworkers were there, as well as the staff she'd become acquainted with during her long hospital stay.

She wore a dress she'd purchased just that afternoon, pale aqua with full, flowing lines, and a pink rosebud corsage to grace its simplicity. Hank surprised her with a nosegay of the same pink rosebuds. "Just a corsage isn't enough," he told her, handing her the flowers. "A bride has to carry flowers."

Emily and Lisa wore pretty new dresses, and Timmy and Joey new corduroys and white shirts. Paula had pulled an incredible number of strings to get, on such short notice, a small wedding cake and even a photographer. He took a few pictures of just Jeanne and Hank and then, becoming more attuned to the atmosphere of the gathering, used the rest of the film for what turned out to be lovely candid shots of them surrounded by some or all of the children.

When the champagne was served, Paula's husband, Al, made just the right toast, simple and direct.

"To your future!" he said happily, and they all raised their glasses, even the six kids, whose festive crystal flutes contained white grape juice.

They spent the night at Paula and Al's. Thoughtfully, Paula had put Jeanne's overnight things in the small room she'd occupied during her convalescence. Hank had the other spare room, and the kids' sleeping bags were spread out on the family-room floor.

Having spent a frantic two days in preparation, they were ready to leave for the ranch the next morning. The van was loaded—*really* loaded. Jeanne was taking all of her and Emily's clothing, all of the toys, the items in the apartment that were uniquely theirs—favorite quilts, pictures, kitchen utensils—and her sewing machine. And the maple rocking chair that belonged first to her grandmother, then to her mother. Jeanne could dimly remember being held by her mother and rocked in that chair. Luckily, practical Aunt Irene had insisted that it be saved when Jeanne's parents' possessions were sold.

Jeanne had turned over the remaining contents of the apartment to the couple across the hall, who had helped her with marketing and errands when Emily was born, and again when she came home from Paula's after the accident.

Also packed in the van were the contents of an exhausting all-day shopping expedition. After their decision Tuesday evening to marry, Hank had said as they drove to Paula's to pick up Emily, "Listen, I know this doesn't sound very romantic, but we need to go shopping tomorrow. Make a list. Write down every single thing you can think of we might need to run a house for several months—including Christmas. Everything. Then we'll go through it and I'll tell you what's already there and what isn't, and we'll go shopping."

Jeanne gasped. "You mean I won't even be able to get to town before Christmas?"

Hank hastily reassured her. "Oh, we'll plan on a trip to Spokane before Christmas. But you can't always count on the weather. If a big whopper of a storm hits, we could get snowed in."

"Hmm," Jeanne murmured, "that sounds like fun. Kind of like *Little House on the Prairie*."

Hank breathed a sigh of relief, then chuckled. "Fun? You must be crazy. But I'm glad the idea isn't sending you running."

So the van was crammed with bulky parcels shrouded in black garbage bags—the result of an adults-only trip to a discount toy store. And clothing for all the kids, with more for Lisa than the rest. "Spandex pants?" Hank said in confusion. "And ten pairs of tights, two of each color? And hot-pink snowboots?"

As Lisa eyed her father anxiously, Jeanne said, "Trust me, Hank, I know what I'm doing."

"Yeah, trust her, Daddy, she knows what she's doing," Lisa echoed.

Jeanne sent Hank away at the door to the fabric store, then hurriedly skimmed through the pattern book and yardage racks. When he came back to pick her up, she said nervously, "It won't always be this expensive, Hank, it's just that getting started—"

"No problem!" he interrupted, patting her cheek. "I notice you've bought nothing for yourself, not even a romance novel. You're doing for the kids what they've really never had anyone do before—being a mother to them."

Mildly intoxicated from the praise and the pat on the cheek, Jeanne groped for a response. "Hmm, I forgot romance novels," she said. "How far from the ranch is the nearest library?"

"Quite a ways," Hank answered seriously, "but when I was a kid Ma made arrangements for books to come by mail from the library in Helena." Then, remembering, "But we're going to stock up on groceries there, too, and they have racks of paperbacks."

At last the van pulled out of Paula and Al's driveway and headed out to the highway that led to Spokane, Helena and points east. Fortunately the van assured all four children of window seats, so most of the trip was accomplished without too much bickering. Lisa was the only child old enough to play license-plate bingo, but even Emily, the youngest, could count animals, so they worked their way through cows, then horses and even ducks, until at last all four of them fell asleep.

That night at the motel Hank asked for a room with two king-size beds. He and the boys shared one bed, Jeanne and the girls the other. He tactfully had his face turned to the wall, feigning sleep, when Jeanne came out of the bathroom in her flannel pajamas. The same scenario was repeated Saturday night.

Just before noon on Sunday, they pulled into Hank's mother's driveway in Helena, and the restless children piled out of the van. Her new mother-in-law won Jeanne's heart immediately by pulling little Emily into the circle of grandchildren. The fact that her daughter had no grandma had always troubled Jeanne. Now it appeared that Emily had one.

Their visit was short. Mrs. Gustafson kept the four children while Jeanne and Hank visited the supermarket, miraculously managing to find room in the van for the groceries. Hank's mother kissed them all goodbye before they set out for the last leg of their journey. As she hugged Jeanne, she whispered, "Since you don't have a mother of your own, maybe someday you'll feel comfortable calling me Ma, like Al, Hank and Paula do." Then she kissed Jeanne. "I'm so glad Hank has someone to love. He's been very lonely."

Jeanne kissed Ma Gustafson's withered cheek with a whispered thank you. Someone to love? Doesn't she know this is a business deal? Jeanne wondered with a twinge of sadness.

The sadness faded in the excitement of nearing her new home. "Only sixty miles more," Hank called out to the kids.

"Sixty miles? I thought we were almost there!" Timmy moaned. But the miles flew by as they took turns telling Jeanne and Emily about the ranch. In Glendora, the last small town before home, Lisa asked her father to drive past her school so Jeanne could see it, and she smiled with satisfaction as Jeanne made appropriately impressed noises. Soon they were slowing for the curving drive up into the Rocky Mountain foothills, with the children pointing out landmarks on the way: the three big side-by-side grain elevators that marked the end of what they called the Flat, the forestry department's water tower, a lightning-blasted pine, curious little shelters alongside the gravel road, with narrow lanes leading into the hillside behind them.

"Those are where kids wait for the school bus," Lisa explained importantly. Jeanne shuddered, picturing lonely Lisa, with frostbitten hands and cheeks, huddled inside a shelter waiting for a broken-down school bus that never arrived. As if reading her mind, Lisa reassured her. "Daddy drives me down in the Jeep and waits with me till the bus comes."

Finally they approached a mailbox and shelter that, according to the three Gustafson children's excited shouts, was theirs. Hank stopped and emptied the mailbox, opened the gate and drove through, then returned and pulled it shut behind them. Climbing back into the van, he glanced nervously at Jeanne, already fearing her reaction. "Not much farther," he said.

At last the moment came. They topped the final rise and the house stood ahead of them. Jeanne suddenly found herself with tears in her eyes. She turned to Hank impulsively. "Those old trees...that tire swing...that long veranda with a swing... Oh, Hank, all the time I was growing up I wanted to live in a house like that...in a *home* like that! Look, there's even smoke coming from the chimney!"

Hank watched her, a wide smile on his face. "Yep, I called Ben and asked them to be sure the place was warm and tidy." Seeing Jeanne's confusion, he added, "Ben's the hired man. His wife, Nora, has helped out when I was in over my head."

"Like when we all had strep throats," Lisa filled in.

With a little crunch of gravel Hank pulled up under the now leafless grape arbor at the back of the house. "We're home!" he called out unnecessarily. "Everybody grab something to carry in!"

By the time darkness fell the van was emptied, and the children had conducted a tour of the house for Jeanne and Emily, as well as checked on the well-being of their dog, cat and horse. Nora brought over a pot of chicken and dumplings and was heartily thanked

for how tidy and inviting the house was. Finally the
children were all bathed and in pajamas. Timmy and
Joey, too tired to protest going to bed, climbed under
the patchwork quilts in their room. Lisa started into
her room, then stopped, a big smile on her face. "Now
I have a sister to share my room! I don't have to sleep
by myself anymore. C'mon, Emily, which side do you
want?"

Emily hesitated for a moment, obviously overwhelmed by so many changes in such a short time.
"Maybe she should sleep with her mama for a little
while, Lisa," her father said, "till she gets used to being in a new place."

Well, thought Jeanne, *you don't have to hit me over
the head with a two-by-four. I get the picture.* A little
relieved to postpone the awkwardness of climbing into
bed with a man who was still a relative stranger, she
nevertheless felt rejected, as though he had leapt at the
chance to decide the time wasn't right. Sweetly she
said, "How very thoughtful, Hank," and extended
her hand to Emily. "Come on to bed with Mommy,
Em."

Their little room was cold. Jeanne investigated and
found that the heat register was closed. She opened it,
then got both herself and her daughter ready for bed.
She climbed under the covers with Emily, gasping at
the touch of the icy sheets.

Jeanne thought of Hank in the big bedroom down
the hall. Was he thinking of *her?* she wondered sleep-
ily. Or was he just feeling relieved that now he
wouldn't have to carry the whole load alone? During
the ride from Helena to the ranch she had daydreamed about a storybook happily-ever-after life,
where they trooped out like the Waltons to cut their

own Christmas tree, and decorated it together. She had pictured the two of them filling stockings by lamplight after all the children were asleep, then climbing the stairs arm in arm to their bedroom.

What was it Aunt Irene had said when she felt Jeanne was getting a bit "uppity," as she put it? Ah, yes. "Just be satisfied with what you have, young lady. There are princesses and there are plain folks, and don't you forget you're plain folks!" Jeanne drifted off to sleep reminding herself to be thankful for what she had, instead of dreaming of what she wanted.

Five

Jeanne awoke confused and disoriented. The room was completely dark, and for a moment she couldn't remember where she was. In a hospital bed, or in Paula's spare room? When she again heard the muffled clanking sound that had awakened her, she threw back the covers and leapt out of bed. Good Lord, it can't be later than two or three in the morning! she thought, but a glance at the illuminated face of the bedside clock showed that it was, in fact, five. Leaving Emily asleep, she hurried to the head of the stairs and looked down.

There was Hank, fully dressed, building a fire in the big iron kitchen range. She felt a moment of panic as she thought of trying to cook on the monster, then remembered the electric stove on the far wall of the kitchen. "We lose our electricity quite often during big storms, so when the folks modernized the kitchen this stayed," Hank had explained. "The fireplace in the living room has a heatilator, and between the two of them the whole downstairs stays pretty warm even without the oil furnace in the cellar."

Jeanne rushed into the upstairs bathroom, splashed her face with icy water, brushed her teeth, pulled her hair back into a ponytail and dressed quickly in jeans and a flannel shirt, then hurried downstairs. Hank was slipping into a denim, sheepskin-lined jacket. "What time does Lisa's schoolbus come by?" Jeanne asked, filling the percolator with water and reaching for the canister of coffee. "And I was thinking, do you suppose since she's missed several days of school, we should drive her today and talk to the teacher for a minute? Let her know her parents are involved and cooperative, even if she has been absent for a week?"

"Hmm, never occurred to me," Hank replied slowly, looking up at the clock on the wall. "It's only twenty after five...maybe..." He snapped his fingers. "No, I can't go. I told Ben last night we'd take the truck into Hawk Valley and haul back that damned busted baler, get it under cover before it snows, so we can work on it."

"Before it snows? Already? It's only November." Jeanne stared at him, a scoop of coffee poised above the percolator.

Hank smiled. "Honey, this isn't Seattle. We often have snow way before Thanksgiving."

Jeanne shook her head, grinning, savoring the "honey." She said, "Well, give me time. I'm just a...a...tenderleg."

Hank gave a snort of laughter. "Tenderleg! I think you mean 'tenderfoot,' Jeanne!"

"Oh, hush! It's rude to laugh at a tenderleg." Then she turned serious. "I can take Lisa down. It's at least three hours before school starts." She slid the coffee onto the burner and headed for the refrigerator. Returning with a slab of bacon and a carton of eggs, she asked, "How far away is this Hawk Valley place? Do you come back in for lunch or should I pack you one?''

Hank sank into a chair by the table, rolled his eyes toward the ceiling and laughed. ''I've died and gone to heaven!'' Then he looked at her and said, ''We should be back by lunchtime, but it'd be great if you made some sandwiches out of that ham Ma sent home with us, and a big thermos of coffee. That way, if it takes longer than we think, we're prepared.'' He got up and headed for the door. ''Could you make a couple extra for Ben? Nora's been sending both of us our lunch for over three years now. I'll go tell her she doesn't need to today.'' He plopped his hat on and started out the door, then stuck his head back in. ''I want to tell you...uh...you look damned pretty there!''

''Does this extra appeal come from the bacon in my left hand or the eggs in my right?'' Jeanne asked innocently. ''What's that old saying, 'The way to a man's heart is through his stomach'?''

Hank groaned. ''I knew it wouldn't come out right. What I meant is you look cute in a ponytail and a flannel shirt—like you're just headed for a 4-H cattle judging or something. Not many women look perky and cute at five in the morning.''

Jeanne waved toward the door. ''Oh, go on. You're forgiven. And thank you.''

When Hank returned a few minutes later with two big jugs of milk, the sizzle of frying bacon and hash browns greeted him. Six half-made sandwiches were lined up on the counter, and the big thermos was filled with hot water, tempering. Jeanne pointed at the milk with her knife. ''Where'd that come from?''

Hank turned to put the jugs in the refrigerator, answering over his shoulder, "I provide the cows and hay, Ben does the milking, Nora runs the separator, and we all share the milk—and butter and cream." Jeanne nodded, impressed. Maybe farmers don't get rich, but they don't go hungry, she thought. If Emily ever moves into Lisa's room and I move into the master bedroom, maybe we should turn that little nook I slept in last night into an exercise room to take care of all that butter and cream!

Jeanne ate breakfast with Hank, then swung into action as his truck pulled out. Soon all the kids were fed and dressed and ready to go. Lisa had picked out one of the new dresses and matching tights, and Jeanne used the curling iron on the shining hair she had trimmed for the little girl before she'd gone to bed last night. The three younger children looked up, suitably impressed. Emily's eyes were wide. "You're pretty, Lisa," she said admiringly.

"C'mon, kids, time to hit the road," Jeanne called, but as they struggled into jackets, a knock sounded on the kitchen door and Nora stuck her head in.

"Your hubby said you're driving Lisa to school this mornin'," Nora said. "Why not leave the others with me?" Jeanne, with an inward smile at the comfortable, old-fashioned term "hubby," accepted gladly, then followed Lisa out to the Blazer. She grabbed a shiny new lunch box off the counter as they left, and in the car she placed it on Lisa's lap.

"My own lunchbox!" Lisa crowed. "How'd you know I hated school lunch?"

"Because you told me about ninety-five times," Jeanne answered dryly. Lisa opened the box and ex-

amined the contents with little exclamations of pleasure.

"Teeny ham sandwiches with the crusts cut off!"
she said happily. "Carrot and celery sticks, and what's
in this little plastic thing? Ooh, ranch dressing to dip
them in! And cookies! And fruit cocktail!" She closed
the lid reverently. "Jeanne, this lunch is even better
than the ones Allison's mother makes for her. Thank
you a million zillion times!"

"You're welcome a million zillion times," Jeanne
answered. "Now flip open that book and see how
many pages you can read to me on the way to school."
During the long drive from Seattle, Jeanne had realized that if Lisa was having problems in school, they
weren't because of a lack of intelligence. The little girl
was a quick learner, and they had very soon worked
their way through the primer reader and simple math
workbook the teacher had sent along. Jeanne strongly
hoped that as soon as Lisa's new, cared-for appearance was noticed by the other children, she would be-
gin to feel good about herself, and enjoy school.

Although she knew that as a daily event the thirty-
some mile drive through the foothills to Glendora
would be a chore, today it was a special treat. The firs
and pines farther up the hillsides were smudges of deep
green, the aspens lining the road had shed their leaves,
making a deep golden carpet beneath the trees. The
sky was like a huge overturned blue bowl. Whenever
she could safely remove her attention from the gravel
road, Jeanne gazed at the panorama surrounding her.
It was no wonder people called this Big Sky Country.
It made you realize there had to be a God.

Once at school, Lisa led Jeanne to her classroom and up to the teacher's desk. "Miss Clark, this is my new mother," she announced proudly.

"How wonderful to meet you!" Miss Clark said, holding her hand out to Jeanne. "It's so nice to have you back, Lisa—and I see you have a lovely new hairdo."

Lisa beamed. "My mother did it."

Jeanne chatted with the teacher for a moment about Lisa's progress through the books she had taken on the trip, then bent and gave Lisa a hug. "I'll meet the bus this afternoon, honey," she said.

Six

The days fell into a hectic sort of pattern. Jeanne mentally ate all the wicked, envious words she'd ever said about stay-at-home moms. It was no picnic. Still, except for the wistful wish that her husband was something more than a friend and business partner, she was happier than she could ever remember being. The college romance with Emily's father hadn't been happiness, she realized now, but just wild infatuation. A sort of puppy love. She felt as though this was where she belonged, where she was meant to be.

She was kept busy cooking and cleaning, of course, but found time to settle on the couch with the kids for stories. Tim, at five, should have been in kindergarten, but because of the long bus ride his father had decided to keep him home. Jeanne hoped that with activities she could enable him to keep pace with the other children when he started first grade next year. She was glad for the television satellite dish Hank had installed on the hillside above the house several years earlier. "Sesame Street" wasn't kindergarten, but it would help.

Tim was also a very handy extra pair of legs and hands, and Jeanne was able to tie in counting, letter recognition and vocabulary with many of his tasks. "Please bring me five potatoes from the pantry, Tim," she would say, holding up five fingers, or, flinging open the cupboard door, "See if you can find three things here that start with the 'buh' sound, Timmy, like 'buh-acon' or . . ."

"Bacon's in the refrigerator," Tim would answer sensibly.

"But look for other things," Jeanne would insist, and soon Tim would spot the can of baked beans, or the picture of biscuits on the box of baking mix.

Hank came in for lunch during one of these letter games, as Tim called them. He looked at Jeanne quizzically. She turned the heat off under the clam chowder and explained, "It's a phonetic letter-recognition activity."

"It is?" Timmy asked in surprise, looking over his shoulder from the utility stool where he was perched. "I thought it was a game."

"Oh, it *is* a game," Jeanne assured him. "Hey, if you're looking for 'puh,' you shouldn't've missed that red-and-black can right in front of your nose."

"Puh-pepper!" the little boy crowed. "Hi, Daddy! I'm looking for 'puhs.'"

Hank hung his hat on the hook by the back door. "You're awfully smart, as well as puh-pretty," he said to Jeanne, as he headed for the utility sink in the corner.

She set aside the "puh-pretty" to think about later. "Oh, I've read my share of yuppie women's magazines," she answered, setting out the soup bowls. "Tim's going to be able to give those city slickers a run for their money when he starts school, aren't you?"

She ruffled the little boy's blond hair, reaching past him for crackers.

Tim lost all interest in finding "puhs." Excitedly, he asked, "Do we run for money at school? How much money? I'm a pretty good runner!"

Jeanne and Hank both chuckled, and Hank slipped his arm around her waist in a little hug before stepping to the door to call Joey and Emily for lunch. Jeanne quickly grabbed the pitcher of orange juice from the refrigerator, wondering if the rivets in her jeans waistband were going to leave scorch marks.

Since Nora had turned over a basically clean house to her, Jeanne was soon able to start sewing during the children's afternoon nap. A small room just off the kitchen, piled full of boxes, empty suitcases and strange odds and ends, intrigued her. She asked Hank about it after lunch one day, and he stood in the doorway with her. "Back in the good old days, when every farm wife had at least one hired girl, this was where she slept," he explained, "close to the kitchen, so she could get the fire built and the kitchen warmed up every morning before anybody else got up."

"Sheesh!" Jeanne exclaimed. "Servants in America?"

"Well, sure," Hank continued seriously. "There'd be a little pile of rags there in the corner for her to sleep on, and a little table over there where she could eat her bread crusts...or was it gruel... Oof!" Jeanne had elbowed him lightly in the ribs, and he gripped the doorjamb, grimacing and moaning till her face showed a tiny bit of alarm, then laughing. "And what do you have in mind for this room?"

"Since you ask," Jeanne began, "here's what I'd like to do." She took a few steps into the room, pulling him with her. "First I'd get rid of all this stuff, then I'd paint the walls yellow or cream. I'd bring down the braided rug from the empty back bedroom upstairs, and make some bright checked curtains." She looked over her shoulder to see if he was paying attention. He was. "Then I'd put my sewing machine there by the window, and on that back wall I'd make shelves out of planks and bricks and have the kids bring all their toys down and keep them here." She was gesturing excitedly now, and he seemed to enjoy just watching her. "Then I'd bring that daybed down from the attic and make a cover for it to match the curtains, and a bunch of puffy pillows, and that's where kids could rest when they're sick." She turned to him, and he quickly smoothed his hand over his grin.

"You've been in the attic?" he asked.

"Well, sure," she said, a bit defensively. "If I'm going to make this the most comfortable home I can, then I have to know the potential." She looked at him sternly. "You're laughing at me!"

He pulled her into his arms and rested his cheek on her soft brown hair. "I'm not laughing at you, honey. I just get a kick out of seeing you get so fired up. I've never heard anybody talk so fast!"

Her arms were shyly reaching up of their own accord to encircle his neck when Tim burst into the room behind his father. "I just saw Ben already starting out to the field with the wire and stuff!" he said importantly.

Jeanne reluctantly stepped out of Hank's arms. He put on his jacket and hat and headed out. Watching him plod through the barren square where she had already planned a kitchen garden for next spring,

Jeanne wondered, certainly not for the first time, what her husband actually felt and thought.

While her feelings for him grew every day, he seemed good-naturedly unaffected. When his hand accidentally touched hers passing dishes at the table, she felt the touch to her very core, while he reminded Timmy not to chew with his mouth open. The night they met in the upstairs hallway, both headed for the bathroom from their individual bedrooms, she was immediately conscious of her breasts free from a bra, touching the flannel of her plaid nightgown. He bowed, gestured to the bathroom doorway and said with a grin, "Ladies first."

He teased her, said nice things to her and playfully put his arms around her, but what did those things really mean? He did those same things with all the children, and even the old dog, Jake. Oh, great! she thought. Isn't that just wonderful for the ego? Maybe he'll get me a flea collar for Christmas!

Seven

As Jeanne stood at the kitchen window watching Hank stride across the stubbled field, remembering the feel of his arms holding her close, she was brought back to earth by a hand tugging at her shirttail. "I don't feel so good, Jeanne," a small voice said.

"Oh, Joey, you don't look so good, either," she said, laying the back of her hand across his forehead. "You're pale, and I think you have a fever. Are you going to...." Yep, he was definitely going to. She grabbed him up and raced to the bathroom.

"I *hate* frowin' up," Joey complained later, as she buttoned him into a pair of fresh pajamas, "and my head hurts!"

By late afternoon Joey still hadn't managed to keep any liquid down, and Jeanne was sponging his forehead, arms and legs with alcohol and cool water. "Tim, would you run over to Nora's and ask her if she could drive down to meet Lisa's bus?" she asked. "Hurry, honey. Or if she'd rather stay here with Joey, I'll drive down, tell her."

When Hank came in that evening, beans were simmering on the stove, instead of the usual meat-and-potatoes dinner. Jeanne had been able to snatch a few minutes to get them started while Joey slept fitfully. Now he was awake again, lethargically resting his head on her breast while she rocked him.

Hank leaned over the pair and laid his cold hand on Joey's hot forehead. "I'm sick, Daddy," the little boy said.

"You sure are, fella." Hank shrugged out of his coat. "Just let me go wash up and I'll take him for a while," he told Jeanne.

"No!" Joey cried fretfully. "Not you, Daddy. Jeanne rocks better."

"You're gonna hurt Daddy's feelings, Joey," his big sister said reproachfully.

"No, that doesn't hurt my feelings, Lisa," Hank assured her. "Joey's no dummy. Of course Jeanne rocks better." He went to the kitchen to wash up and see what he could do to finish dinner. Watching his retreating back, Jeanne was almost grateful that for a few days, at least, she wouldn't keep halfway expecting some action from him that would move their marriage out of neutral, and then be disappointed when nothing occurred. At least she knew where she was and what was expected of her: taking care of sick children.

By the time Joey was able to keep down gelatin and ginger ale, Tim was feeling sick. Just like clockwork, Emily went down next. Then, surprising even himself, Hank. Followed by Lisa. Hank was just beginning to feel halfway human again when Jeanne paled and ran for the bathroom.

All in all, it was not a time that memories are made of. The marginally well ones helped each other as long as possible. Ben took over all the ranch chores, and Nora came by several times a day with soup and aspirin, hurrying out again as quickly as possible. On what felt like the ninth or tenth or seventieth day, Jeanne raised her head from the living-room couch where she lay, counted the children listlessly watching cartoons on TV, took a sip of flat soda, and lowered her head to the pillow again. "Do you suppose this is what it was like during the Black Plague, whole families...uh...sick at the same time?" she asked nobody in particular. Actually, "whole families *dying* at the same time" had been more like it, she knew, but she didn't want to scare the kids.

"Probably," came a disembodied voice from behind the couch. Hank was there, napping on the floor, covered with a quilt. "Shall I go see if Nora's painted a big black *X* on the door?"

"Nah, never mind," Jeanne answered. "Who cares?"

"Bet you wish you were back in Seattle."

"Flu's flu, no matter where you are. At least here there's plenty of company when you're sick. Do you have the box of tissues back there?"

Hank pulled himself up and handed it to her. Leaning down, he brushed a wisp of hair off her forehead. Her nose was red-tipped, her lips were chapped, and dark shadows ringed her eyes. He frowned fiercely.

Jeanne gazed up at him, reading in his expression that she looked a real sight. "Well, you're no Prince Charming yourself right now!" she snapped, then turned on her side, face to the back of the couch.

"I didn't say a word!" Hank said, amazed.

"Well, you thought it!"

He chuckled. "Does this mean the honeymoon's over—reading my mind and bawling me out for what I'm thinking?"

"Hah! What honeymoon?"

He pulled the afghan up over her shoulders and let his fingers linger a moment on her cheek, then crossed to the fireplace to put another log in. He brushed the bark dust from his hands and headed for the back porch.

"Don't get chilled when you're just getting over the flu," Jeanne called as she heard the back door open.

"No, I won't. Just getting more wood." He brought an armload, laid it gently in the wood box in case any of the kids were sleeping and brushed off his chest. He lifted Jeanne's feet, laid them on his lap and tucked the afghan under them carefully.

She opened her eyes and gazed at him for a moment. "What day is it?"

"I don't know. Let's see . . ." He stared into space, obviously trying to find an event to hang a date on. "Uh, I think it's Wednesday. Why? You going someplace?"

"No, just trying to figure out how many days of school Lisa has missed."

"Heard on TV that Glendora schools have been closed for a couple of days. Fifty-percent absenteeism. Guess we're not the only sick family."

"Good. I mean, not good, somebody else is sick, but good, Lisa won't be far behind the rest of the class." Then she fell asleep.

Eight

In a few days they were all in various stages of recovery. Jeanne noticed that Hank's fingers seemed to linger on hers longer than necessary in the usual "Please pass the carrots" transaction, and that he sometimes kissed her cheek as he left for his outside work.

Defiantly she pushed Aunt Irene's "princesses and plainfolks" rule into the far recesses of her mind and allowed herself to dream again.

On a gray afternoon she stood at the sink gazing out the window at the empty landscape, peeling Winesaps for applesauce, toying with a wonderful fantasy. It had Hank stealing into her tiny bedroom in the middle of the night when the children were sleeping, picking her up and carrying her down the hall to the master bedroom, the frothy pink lace of her satin nightgown spilling over his strong arms. Just as the knowledge that she didn't even own a satin nightgown brought the daydream to a standstill, the Jeep pulled up and Ben beckoned to her urgently.

Instead of carrying Jeanne down the hall to the bedroom, Hank was carried into the house on a makeshift stretcher by Ben, Nora and Jeanne, had his ankle temporarily splinted by Jeanne, then rode down the mountain to the doctor's office in the back seat of Ben's big old '72 Buick. He was not a jolly passenger.

"How could I be so stupid?" he muttered, clenching his teeth when Ben hit a bump. "Stepping in a gopher hole! Damn!"

Jeanne turned around to soothe him from the front passenger seat. "It could've been worse, Hank. Just think, if you'd been riding Molly and she'd stepped in it, she'd probably have a broken leg and you'd have Lord knows what broken!"

Ben said seriously, "You listen to your wife, man. She's right." He snickered. "'Course, Molly's too smart to step in a gopher hole!"

"I heard that, buddy!" Hank said through gritted teeth. "Lucky for you I've got to be nice to you no matter what you say, because I doubt I'll be out riding any fences for a week or two."

"A week or two?" Jeanne said to Ben in a stage whisper. "More like a month or two, at least."

She was right. Hank had broken three bones in his ankle. The doctor kept him in Glendora's little six-bed emergency clinic overnight just to be safe, and the next day Ben and Jeanne drove back down to bring him home. He hobbled to the car with a cast and crutches, and with instructions to stay off his feet for a month.

"Well, look on the bright side," Jeanne said calmly. "At least you don't have to punch a time clock, and you won't get your wages docked for being off work."

Hank grabbed his knee to pull his leg in, threw his crutches on the floor and heaved a big gusty sigh. "May the good Lord protect me from a Pollyanna!" he snarled.

Jeanne slammed his door and climbed in the front seat. "Well, pardon *me!*" she snapped, and slammed her own car door.

"I'm sorry, Jeanne. Just don't be... don't be so damned cheerful, if you can help it," Hank apologized lamely.

Jeanne sniffed.

Ben started the car. "Now I don't want to interfere, but remember this old boat is more 'n twenty years old. Another coupla slams like that and she might just fall into a pile of rust and bolts!"

Jeanne turned her head for a quick peek at Hank, and they both started to laugh. "No more slams," Hank guaranteed.

Even though Ben was doing all the ranch work, Hank's day, and thus Jeanne's, still began early. The two men had coffee in the kitchen while they went over Ben's plans for the day. Ben could have managed fine without the consultation, and Jeanne appreciated his thoughtfulness in letting Hank feel he was still running the ranch.

The first few days after she had arrived from Seattle, Jeanne had moaned when the alarm went off each morning, but soon her body accepted the new schedule; the changing shifts of her hospital nursing job had prepared her for a quick adjustment. Now that Hank was confined to the house, the quiet time before the children awoke was very pleasant. They were getting to know one another in a depth that would have taken much longer with Hank spending his days out on the ranch. Sometimes they had a peaceful breakfast together; sometimes one or more of the children joined them.

Often Emily became aware of her mother's absence in bed and padded down the stairs. Jeanne sensed that her daughter loved being around Hank. She had often regretted Emily's not knowing a father's affection, so seeing the bond growing between her daughter and Hank was deeply satisfying.

One evening when Emily took an "ouchie" to her stepfather instead of her mother, Jeanne was moved almost to tears at the sight of the little girl sitting on Hank's lap, trustingly holding her palm up to him so he could search for the splinter. He found it, and Jeanne brought the tweezers and alcohol. "This might hurt a little, honey," Hank warned. "Are you tough?"

Emily nodded seriously. "I'm very tough." She clenched her teeth, then gave a big sigh of relief when the sliver came out. Hank hugged her, and she sat quietly on his lap for a few minutes before joining Tim and Joey and the Lego village they were building, sure that it was only a matter of time before they eclipsed the structure they had seen at Seattle Center. Hank reached for his newspaper, and his eyes met Jeanne's. The smile she gave him was tender.

One afternoon when Tim, Joey and Emily were napping, Hank called Jeanne into the den, where he did the record-keeping for the ranch. She entered with two mugs of coffee and handed him one. He got right to the point. "Jeanne, I'd like to adopt Emily, if you agree."

"Why...yes. I'm glad you want to do that. I...I've worried about Emily's future ever since the accident."

"Being a ward of the court or having foster parents would *legally* take care of Em's future, Jeanne. But how do you feel about having me be her *father?*"

Jeanne looked at him soberly for a moment. "I don't think anyone could be a better father, Hank," she said softly, meaning it with all her heart. He worked hard for the children and made time for them even when he was tired. He treated all four of them with equal attention and affection. Someday she would tell him so, but for now she just said, "You're a great dad."

"Good. I'll call the lawyer who handles the ranch business and have him find out how we go about it." Reaching for the phone, he paused for a sip of coffee. "Seems like I read somewhere that you have to put a legal notice in the newspaper a certain number of times, giving the natural parent a chance to respond." He took another sip. "Good coffee."

"Wait," Jeanne said quickly. "Before you call, what about the other kids?"

He looked at her, puzzled. "What about them?"

"What if something happened to you? Would their mother's parents take them?"

"I...I don't know," Hank said. "Cyndi's parents were divorced long ago. Her father hasn't even seen the kids. And you already know about how her mother wrote them out of the picture when Cyndi disappeared." He sat silently for a long moment, gazing into his cup. "I hadn't thought about that. Didn't think anything would ever happen to me, I guess."

"Probably never thought you'd step in a gopher hole and break your ankle in three places, either."

Hank stared out the window at the frosty gray stubble in the nearest field. "In my will, Paula and Al would have custody of the kids." He swiveled back to face her. "Three kids are a big responsibility."

"What if I adopted them? I think they're beginning to think of me as their mother." Jeanne sipped her coffee thoughtfully. "I love them, Hank. Even if something happened to you—*especially* if something happened to you—I'd still want to be their mother."

"Yes. I'd want you to be. Let me see what we have to do."

"But it has to be their choice. Lisa's old enough to remember her mother, and Tim remembers a little, too. I only want to do this if it's what they want."

"All right, we'll talk about it tonight at bedtime." Hank grinned. "That'll be a switch. Instead of reading a fairy tale about a wicked stepmother who sends the children out to get lost in the woods, we'll talk about a sweet stepmother who wants to adopt them. In the meantime, I'll call and find out about the legalities." He swallowed the last of his coffee and reached for the phone again.

Jeanne stood up. "Let me know what he says. I've got to get back to work. I'm almost ready to start on some Christmas projects." As she leaned over Hank to pick up his mug, he caught her hand, pulled it to his mouth and pressed a soft kiss into her warm palm.

She felt electrified. He released her hand, and almost of their own volition, Jeanne's fingertips drifted to his forehead, where the sun-lightened hair waved crisply back. Before she had a chance to think about the wisdom of wanting more than she already had, she bent down and pressed a butterfly kiss right there. Then she turned in confusion, grabbed the mug and hurried from the room. What was happening to her? Was the disciplined woman who was learning all about ranching and mothering and running a household turning into a bowl of jelly?

The murmur of Hank's voice on the telephone followed her down the hall. In the kitchen, she put their cups in the dishwasher and, lost in thought, was gazing out at the gray sky meeting the gray fields when he limped into the room on his crutches. "Sam says it'll be quick and simple for you to adopt the kids," Hank said, leaning against the counter and propping his crutch alongside. "Since their mother is dead, we don't even have to put a notice in the newspaper, giving the natural parent a chance to respond. It'll take a little longer for me to adopt Emily."

"For the advertising in the paper?"

"Yeah. But Sam said he didn't anticipate any problems under the circumstances. We'll have the notice in the paper, and Sam will take care of the paperwork. I told him to draw up a new will, too, including all these changes. Then we'll make a trip to Helena to wrap everything up." He limped to the refrigerator and peered inside. "Are these apples still crisp?"

"I think so. I had one yesterday and it was okay." She moved to the open refrigerator. "Not the Delicious, though. They're past their prime. Try one of the Granny Smiths."

Hank took an apple, found the salt shaker in the cupboard, retrieved his crutch and started back to the den. "You know where I am if you need me," he said around a mouthful of apple.

Jeanne watched her husband limp down the hallway. So they would all be a family, as she'd dreamed. But did Hank's moment of tenderness allow her to include in that fantasy family a husband and wife who loved each other?

Nine

Hank's mother called regularly once a week just to "stay in touch." Jeanne was pleasantly surprised that from the very beginning, Mrs. Gustafson had never immediately asked to talk to her son, but chatted with Jeanne until Jeanne herself broke off the conversation to get Hank.

Mrs. Gustafson had invited them to spend Thanksgiving at her home in Helena, and everyone, for their different reasons, was looking forward to the trip.

Tim, Joey and Lisa couldn't wait to visit Grandma. The two boys had filled Emily's head with so many exciting details about their grandmother and her house that Jeanne, overhearing some of the conversations and learning the rest from Emily, could hardly keep a straight face as she relayed them to Hank during breakfast one morning.

"Em must have had jet lag when we stopped in Helena on the way up here, Hank. She doesn't remember too much about your mom's place," she reported, refilling their coffee cups. "She can hardly wait to visit again. From the boys' details, she's expecting a situation sort of like Mary Poppins in charge of a giant toy store."

Hank chuckled. "She'll have fun. Ma and her friend Eunice always hit the yard sales to make sure they've got a good supply of grandkid entertainment."

Lisa's anticipation was for a different reason. One morning as Jeanne was using the curling iron to put a couple of waves on either side of the child's face, Lisa asked, "Jeanne, can I take all the new school clothes you made me to show to Grandma?"

"You're going to have a pretty full suitcase for a four-day visit, honey," Jeanne answered. "Wouldn't you rather just tell her about them?"

"Oh, she'd like to see them, I know," Lisa said to her stepmother's reflection in the mirror. "Before you came, whenever we visited her, she always took us downtown to buy some clothes, even when she didn't feel good." She stretched her lips to inspect the new gap where the first baby tooth had recently come out. "I think Grandma's gonna be glad we have a mom now."

Jeanne unplugged the curling iron and fluffed the waves with her fingers. "There! You're gorgeous!"

Lisa hadn't moved, but still spoke to the reflection in the mirror. "When am I s'posed to call you Mom?" she asked.

"Well, anytime you want to," Jeanne answered. "We started working on adoption after we talked to all of you about your dad adopting Emily and me adopting you and the boys. I just don't want to rush you, though, and make you think you *have* to call me Mom."

"It's not 'cause I *have* to. It's 'cause I want to... Mom."

Jeanne thought for a moment her heart would burst. Then she wondered if Emily would be jealous when she heard the other children calling her Mom. Her doubts were settled a few minutes later when all the children piled into the Blazer to take Lisa down the hill to the bus stop and wait with her there.

"Em," said Lisa conversationally, "would you like to be my sister?"

"I already *am* your sister."

"Not really," Lisa said, with the authoritative wisdom that the three-year age difference allowed her. "We're really just stepsisters till we're adopted, but if I give you my dad and you give me your mom, *then* we're sisters."

"Okay." Seemed like a reasonable deal to Emily—and to the little boys, who had listened to the exchange and were quite secure in the knowledge that their big sister knew everything in the world there was to know. So Jeanne had become "Mom" to Lisa, Tim and Joey, although Joey often called her Mommy, as Emily did, especially when he was tired. Lisa, Jeanne knew, could hardly wait for her grandma to know that Jeanne really *was* their new mom.

For his part, Hank had declared he looked forward to the visit so that he and Jeanne could have a little time away from the kids. He knew he'd be able to count on his mother to watch them while he and Jeanne went out to dinner and a movie.

As for Jeanne, she *needed* that trip to Helena. She needed to be a little removed from the four walls that held together six people who were a family, and yet, in one important regard—the parents' physical intimacy—were not.

On this frosty November morning Jeanne sat idly at her sewing machine, watching through the newly-curtained window as Hank hobbled toward the barn on his crutches. She had always thought marriages of convenience were a thing of the past. Now she was living one. Often, after an evening of reading, watching television or playing Scrabble with Hank, Jeanne longed to simply walk into his room with him and climb into bed. Each time, though, she remembered the distant stare he sometimes had, as though he were a million miles away—with someone else. For her own pride and self-respect, she wouldn't make the first move. As he'd said back in Seattle, they were both healthy adults and they'd know when the time was right. Except it was beginning to seem it never would be.

Well, it *was* a marriage of convenience, and she'd best keep that in mind, she reminded herself, and not build some fragile fairy-tale romance that only existed in her mind and then be devastated when it came crashing down around her.

She sat a moment longer looking out the window, watching Hank's breath puff out in little clouds in the cold air. Then she sighed and slid the cornflower-blue corduroy under the needle. It was to be a warm robe for Hank, the exact color of his eyes.

The trip to Helena would be fun. She had called her Seattle bank, where Hank had insisted she leave her savings, and requested a draft be sent to her, so she could do some Christmas shopping to round out what they had bought before they left the city. She hadn't known Hank's children then, so she had purchased generic toys, but now she wanted to buy special things for each child. And she'd like to get herself a few nice things. Maybe a silky nightgown in the dark rose she knew flattered her, and a soft, fluffy robe in the same color. She could put them on after tucking in the kids, and Hank would see her sitting there, firelight glowing on her cheeks, and he'd come over and sit down by her, pull her into his arms, and the robe would slip off one shoulder, revealing the silky gown and her creamy skin...

A pipedream! But she still looked forward to the Thanksgiving trip. Hank's mother would no doubt put them in the same bedroom. Probably nothing would happen. The house was small, the walls thin. And Hank's cast would have put a crimp even into lovemaking between two people with the ease of years between them, with the old-shoe comfort that allowed them the ability to laugh at awkwardness, to improvise. But at least she'd be able to feel his nearness in the night, and pretend he loved her.

At last the day before Thanksgiving arrived. With the suitcases loaded into the van, Hank and Jeanne and the three younger children were waiting in the parking lot when Lisa got out of school. Jeanne drove, and Hank copiloted by body language and sharp little intakes of breath until finally, in exasperation, she gave him a meaningful glare.

"I know how to drive, Hank," she explained a few minutes later, feeling guilty for the glare. She'd seen her aunt use it effectively on Uncle Bert many times, but for the past few miles she'd been remembering that Aunt Irene and Uncle Bert had rarely seemed even friendly to each other. She wondered if the glare had anything to do with it.

"I know you do, Jeanne," Hank answered. He reached over to pat her knee. "It's just that I'm about as bad a passenger as I am a patient."

"Well, surprise, surprise, as Gomer Pyle used to say. For some strange reason I already knew that!"

Darkness was falling as they drove into Ma Gustafson's driveway, and the yellow lamplight of her windows welcomed them. Kids exploded out of the van, with Tim and Joey pulling Emily between them, eager to show her the sights. Ma hurried out, and she and Jeanne helped Hank down on his crutches.

When she entered the house, Jeanne stopped for a moment and took a deep breath. Hank looked at her, a question in his eyes. She laughed shakily. "It's just . . . when I was a kid and daydreamed about having a family like everyone else, this was what Thanksgiving was like." She shook her head. "I'm sorry. It sounds corny, I know. But the smells—" she sniffed appreciatively the combination of faint wood smoke that had drifted in with them, spicy potpourri from the brass dish on the hall table and freshly baked mince and pumpkin pies "—and the kids running in, all excited, and Grandma . . ."

Hank reached out and pulled her into a quick hug. Then he simply stood there, holding her close.

Is he pitying me? Jeanne wondered. Am I just Emily with a splinter, or Joey with a stubbed toe? She didn't move from the shelter of his arms, though, until Tim, Joey and Emily, hand in hand, raced pell-mell down the hall toward them, dropping hands at the last minute to swerve to either side. Hank and Jeanne stepped apart, but Jeanne knew the closeness of that embrace would warm her for a long time—perhaps, she hoped, even till the next time she felt like a wife of convenience.

· The four days seemed to fill all their expectations. Grandma Gustafson was true to Tim and Joey's extravagant advance billing. Her latest yard-sale treasures were stored in the guest-room closet: a tulle-and-net prom dress, sequin-spattered evening gown, a couple of veiled and feathered hats, even an old tux and top hat. She admired Lisa's new wardrobe, read stories to them all, and better still, she listened while Lisa demonstrated her own new recently acquired reading skill.

On Friday, Hank stayed with the kids while Ma and Jeanne went shopping. Jeanne finished her Christmas buying and found all the supplies needed to finish the projects already started. They had a long, leisurely lunch, with no mother-in-law advice or questions.

That night, Ma watched the children while Hank and Jeanne went out to dinner and a movie. In the theater, his arm made a slow but purposeful descent to encircle Jeanne's shoulders, and he pulled her close enough that the warm exhalations of his breath stirred the hair along her temple.

And best of all, they shared the guest-room bed. It was awkward. Oh, yes, it was awkward. It was also worth every shy, uncomfortable minute. They began each night staidly back-to-back, facing opposite walls. When morning came, staidness had departed. The first morning Jeanne awoke still facing her wall, but in his sleep Hank had pulled her close and her back was cradled against his warm chest. The next two mornings the roles were reversed. She was nestled tightly against *his* back. And the last morning, they awoke in each other's arms.

Jeanne had been slowly surfacing into wakefulness, so deliciously comfortable that her body resisted morning. Her internal alarm, accustomed to going off at five o'clock, told her it was much later than that, and the lightness of the room confirmed the feeling. She stirred and was jolted awake by the firmness of Hank's body against hers, by his arm resting over her hip. At her movement, his arm tightened and pulled her closer, though he still slept. Bittersweet emotion flooded through Jeanne as she realized how happy awakening in Hank's arms every morning for the rest of her life would make her. Oh, if only...if only they could have met and loved and then married. If only he loved her, instead of just requiring her services as a housekeeper and her body for his physical needs. If she couldn't have more from him than a certain appreciation and the matter-of-fact sex she knew would be a part of her life soon, then she'd be much better off if she didn't love him. Love. The word lingered bitterly. Yes, she did love him, and she wished she didn't. She wished his touch didn't make her catch her breath and melt inside. She had experienced one-sided love before and felt its pain. She had sworn it would never happen again, and look at her now.

She felt Hank's body stir against her. His hand left her hip and lifted her chin. Their lips met. *If I can't have what I want, then I'll take what I can get,* Jeanne thought, and then stopped thinking, lost in the kiss.

The bedroom door was flung open. "Daddy, Daddy, it's snowing!" Joey shouted, running to the bed. Then, conversationally, "Were you kissin'?"

"Can we build a snowman, Dad?" Now Tim was in the room, too. "Mom, Grandma told me she's makin' Dutch babies for breakfast. Do I hafta eat 'em? Dutch babies!" he ended in horror.

Hank moaned softly. "First thing when we get home, I'm putting a lock on the bedroom door," he whispered to Jeanne as she threw back her side of the patchwork quilt and leapt out of bed, giving him a small, uncertain smile as she did so.

"First breakfast, then a snowman." She grabbed her robe and moved Tim and Joey briskly ahead of her. "Tim, you'll love Dutch babies," she assured him. "You like applesauce and puffy pancakes, don't you?"

Hank listened as their voices moved away down the hall. "Well, yeah," Tim responded slowly. "But if it's just pancakes 'n' applesauce, why's it called Dutch babies? That's gross."

"I don't know," Jeanne answered. "Maybe little Dutch babies love it. Or maybe a Dutch baby spilled his applesauce on his daddy's pancake one morning, and his daddy took one taste of it, and said..."

The kitchen was full of laughter and the mouth-watering aroma of frying bacon. Jeanne slid a puffy pancake onto Hank's plate and he sniffed appreciatively. "Hank, do you think if we stopped in Glendora the doctor would put the lighter cast on?" She stepped to the stove and pulled the pan off the burner, having seen that Ma was tired and needed a break. "He told us to come back around the first of December, and this is pretty close to it."

Hank spread warm applesauce on half his pancake and poured syrup on the other half. "Maybe he would," he said. "It's Sunday, but he's usually around the clinic in the afternoon."

"Well, then, you kids had better hurry with your snowman," Ma reminded them. "You'll want to be in Glendora no later than three-thirty or four at the latest."

Ten

As she negotiated the steep lane and parked by the back door, Jeanne felt a thrill of homecoming. She marveled that after less than two months, the weather-beaten old farmhouse in its stand of cottonwood and oak seemed to hold out welcoming arms to her.

Jeanne heated the homemade turkey noodle soup Ma had sent home with them and made grilled cheese sandwiches, while Hank, with his lighter cast and one crutch, started a fire in the kitchen range and then supervised the two bath sessions. Tim and Joey were out of their shared tub and into pajamas in jig time. When Lisa called that she and Emily were ready to get out, Hank went in for the ritual inspection of necks and ears, although it really wasn't necessary. Lisa, in the big-sister role she so enjoyed, always made sure that Emily bathed properly.

A few minutes later, they were all seated around the kitchen table eating while the sticks of pine in the stove snapped crisply. Emily intently chased a plump homemade noodle up the side of her bowl, finally maneuvering it into her spoon. Then she looked up brightly and announced, "Me and Lisa are going to tell Christmas secrets in our room."

"Oh, are you and Lisa going to share a room now?" Jeanne asked.

"Yep," Emily answered. "Daddy said we could."

Jeanne's eyes met Hank's over the children's heads. He smiled a bit self-consciously and nodded. So, he'd had a talk with the girls when he'd gone to supervise their bathing. And he'd apparently been successful. She suddenly felt a rapid little pulse in her throat that she hadn't noticed before, and was aware of warmth creeping up her cheeks. She hoped Hank didn't see it.

While she tucked the kids in for the night, he put the dishes into the dishwasher and lit the kindling already arranged in the living-room fireplace. When she emerged after settling the noise level in the boys' room, the mellow sound of Phil Collins drifted up the stairs from the stereo. Jeanne hesitated a moment, then took a quick shower and slipped into her flannel pajamas. Now that she finally had the silky rose nightgown, she hesitated to wear it. It would look so...so *calculated,* as though she expected a big romantic event, she thought ruefully. And while she might hunger for a tender, emotional beginning that worked toward a passionate finish, it was not what she expected. Still...oh, what the heck! She could at least wear the robe!

She picked up the book from her nightstand and started downstairs, feeling the music swirl around her and into her senses.

Hank stood at the fireplace, back to the stairs and poker in hand. He turned and grinned at her as she sat down on the couch. "Sounded there for a while like the boys got a second wind."

"And a third and a fourth," Jeanne replied. "I think the idea of Christmas secrets being told in the next room drove them crazy." She pulled a cushion under her elbow. "They evidently figured if they couldn't beat the girls at telling Christmas secrets, they could win with sheer volume." Jeanne shivered slightly. The new pink robe might look great, but it wasn't much for warmth.

Hank leaned his crutch against the couch and lowered himself beside her. Putting his arm around her, he drew her near. "Cold?" he asked. "Takes this old place a long time to heat up after the thermostat has been turned down for a few days."

I think romance, he thinks thermostat! Aunt Irene's words again rang in Jeanne's mind. "Be satisfied with what you've got."

His other arm came around her, too, and he pulled her closer, till her head was against his chest. She let it rest there, listening to the strong, steady thrum of his heart. "If it was cold enough to snow in Helena, then it was probably a lot colder than that up here," Jeanne said, finally thinking of a response to his thermostat comment.

Oh, Lord, I sound so stupid! she thought. What am I, Wendy the Weather Girl? I'm trying to be so calm about this…this next step in our arrangement. Maybe he'll never love me, but at least he'll never know that I love him. If I can't save my heart, at least I can save my pride.

Hank stirred. "Let's sit over there by the fire," he said, and stood slowly, his crutch in one hand, Jeanne's hand in the other. He sank into the big leather platform rocker by the fire, and pulled Jeanne down onto his lap. Holding her close, he began to rock.

Jeanne nestled closer. She couldn't help it. The fire was crackling, the wind that had come up whined around the corners of the house, the grandfather clock ticked, soft music from the stereo enveloped them. Hank's arms were strong and gentle at the same time, and she felt more completely safe and cared for than she could ever remember. Hold on to this, she told herself. If this is as good as it's going to get, if this is what I have, instead of romance and passion, okay. This will be good enough. She closed her eyes and relaxed against him.

For a long time they just fitted against each other, quietly rocking in the big chair. Hank's breathing and his hard body against Jeanne revealed his arousal. Although Jeanne knew it signified nothing except that he had been lonely and hungry for a woman's touch for a long time, she was grateful that he left her this illusion of tenderness, that he didn't rush to satisfy his own needs.

Eventually Hank slipped his hand beneath her pajama top and began to slowly stroke her back, from the little knobs at the base of her neck to the elastic of her pajama bottoms, then up to softly massage her neck, around to the tender hollows behind and below each ear. Jeanne whispered something he apparently didn't catch. "What did you say?" he whispered back, leaning down so his ear was near her lips.

"I said, that if I were a cat I'd be purring," Jeanne murmured, opening her eyes and turning her face till their lips met. The kiss was as gentle as the caresses had been. His lips moved to the corners of her mouth, her cheeks, her temples, her closed eyelids, the wildly fluttering pulse at the base of her throat, then back to her mouth. Their lips parted sweetly, and the sound of

Hank's labored breathing joined the other nighttime noises. A tiny moan escaped Jeanne, and Hank struggled awkwardly to his feet.

"I'd like to carry you up to our bedroom," he murmured unsteadily, "but I can't." Instead, he slipped his arm around her waist and they slowly climbed the stairs, stopping often while their lips and bodies met. Once in their room, Hank quietly closed the door behind them.

Afterward, Jeanne could never remember who led whom to the bed and who threw back the quilt. Perhaps it was a joint effort. Undressing certainly was. He opened her pajama top and kissed her taut breasts until her whole body quivered, then slid the elastic waistband of the bottom down over her hips. She unbuttoned his flannel shirt, and while he shrugged it off his shoulders, she struggled with the buckle of his belt and the stubborn metal fasteners of his jeans. He fell back on the bed as she maneuvered the denim over his cast, then pulled her down beside him. In the privacy of their own little haven, it was difficult to know if the sighing moans were the wind whispering around the eaves, or Hank... or Jeanne.

He held her in the circle of his arms until he fell asleep. She lay there in his embrace for a long time before sleep finally took her. She remembered his voice saying, "Oh, Jeanne, Jeanne." But he'd never said, "Oh, Jeanne, Jeanne, I love you."

Eleven

Jeanne stood at the sink, gazing out the kitchen window as she smoothed lotion on her hands. She sighed. The gray of the sky met the brownish-gray of harvested fields and sleeping earth, matching her mood.

This was stupid, she told herself angrily. I should be taking advantage of nap time to work on Christmas projects I can't do while the kids are around. Resolutely she went to her cozy sewing room just off the kitchen and pulled down a box from the top of the storage shelves. Then she stood aimlessly again, rubbing the soft, Santa-printed outing flannel with her fingertips. Two uninterrupted hours would finish the girls' nighties and the boys' pajamas, but she just couldn't seem to get with it today.

She tried a mental pep talk, a variation of the one she'd been giving herself for the past three weeks: You should be grateful, instead of whining. You have a beautiful old house to live in, the kind you always wanted. You have a husband who is good to you and your daughter. His children have accepted you as their mother. Think of how bad it could be. You took a real chance, marrying someone you didn't know and letting him bring you way out in the boonies. He

could've been a Bluebeard . . . or the the home could
have been like the one you grew up in, with nothing
more than cool tolerance between husband and wife.
Instead, there's laughter and affection. He's gentle and
sweet, and considerate of you.

Her hands moved to gather up the partially finished garments, while her mind wandered. And there's
warmth. Oh, yes. Sometimes, lots of warmth. Under
that patchwork quilt there's warmth that blazes up like
a flash fire, until sometimes I could almost think he
loves me. But that's not love—it's lust. He needs
me . . . needs my body, anyway. And I need his just as
much.

She carried the cloth to the sewing machine, sat
down and began pinning eyelet ruffling to the neck of
a nightie. So why can't I just accept what I *do* have?
Why can't I just enjoy the pleasure his passion gives
me and forget about love? But passion isn't enough.
Instead of just a little sip, I want the whole glass. I
want him to love me with his heart and soul. The way
I do him. But he doesn't and probably never will. So
I won't let him know how I really feel. After all, we're
not giddy teenagers. We're two mature adults making
the best of a marriage of convenience.

As if her concentrated thoughts had created him,
through the window she saw Hank limping slowly toward the house, and the giddy teenager instantly
evicted the mature adult. Angry at being betrayed by
her own body, she violently pressed the sewing-
machine pedal. By the time the back door opened, the
steady whir of her machine filled the room. Hank
moved stealthily behind her chair and put his cold
hand on her neck. She gave a little yelp.

"I could use some coffee. How about you?" he said. "Hey, that's pretty snazzy. You're almost finished."

"Almost," Jeanne replied. "Yeah, coffee sounds good. I'll go start a pot."

"No, I'll fix it. You need to make hay while the sun shines. Or the kids sleep. Carry on."

As the coffeepot clinked and the water ran, Jeanne's Pollyanna side took over. *See? See how sweet he is to you?* Then her cynical side spoke up. *Oh, sure. A loaf of bread, a jug of coffee, and thou.* Once again her foot pressed the pedal.

Soon Hank was back with two steaming cups. Carefully placing Jeanne's on the chest beside her, he lowered himself into the maple rocker with a low "Ah-h-h."

"You're not staying off that leg enough."

"No, the leg's fine. It's just that I haven't been on a horse for about six weeks, and my body's reminding me how long it's been."

The whirring of the machine stopped. Jeanne stared at her husband in disbelief. "You were on a horse with that leg? You're crazy!"

"Nah, no big deal. I rode Smoke, the only one lazy enough to stand still while I climb up hay bales and fling my bum leg over his back." He took a sip of coffee. "The truck's great, so's the Blazer, but some places you can only get to with a horse."

Jeanne shook her head in dismay, trying to rid herself of a vision of the horse taking a few steps forward while Hank was "flinging his bum leg over." It was a frightening picture. "Sounds to me like a good way to have two bum legs, instead of just one," she commented dryly.

"No, I'm careful," Hank said cheerfully, then tried to change the subject. "There's a pretty little stand of fir just beyond that ridge you can see from the kitchen window. Got a few Scotch pine and spruce, too. I rode over to check on Christmas trees."

"Wow, cutting our own tree!" Jeanne exclaimed. "Just like a Christmas story! Do we have decorations?"

"Yup, boxes of 'em, up in the attic," Hank assured her. "Since Ma moved to Helena, she has a little pink tree with silver ornaments. Said she'd always wanted one like that." He chuckled. "Pa probably rolls over in his grave every December. He was a great one for tradition. Always had the tree picked out a year or two ahead, a big one. His favorite ornament, a blue glass bird, always had to go in the same place." He was silent for a moment, and when he spoke again his voice was fond. "Pa knew how to celebrate Christmas," he said simply.

"I wish I could have known him."

"I wish you could have, too. Pa would have loved you." He stood stiffly. "Well, I'm rested up. You want to come pick out the tree, or do you trust me?"

"When spring comes I'm going to learn how to ride," Jeanne said firmly, "but for now, you'd better pick one out without me." She glanced at him with a little grin. "Who are we kidding? You've already got it picked out."

Hank nodded sheepishly and headed for the door.

"But take Ben with you!" Jeanne called after him.

"Yes, Mother dear," Hank answered dutifully, already out of the room.

"I'm not your mother," Jeanne growled at the sewing machine.

"And I'm awfully glad you're not!" Hank stuck his head back inside, grinning so lecherously Jeanne couldn't help laughing, even as she threw a package of bias tape at him.

Late that evening, staring almost reverently at the pine he'd cut, Jeanne knew she had never seen such a beautiful tree. It was huge, bushy and fresh, nothing like the city trees she had known. The old glass balls caught the firelight's glow and reflected varied colors from the strings of lights. The children and Hank had trimmed the lower branches, and Jeanne, on a stepladder, had done the higher reaches, putting the angel in place on top. After the kids were in bed, she and Hank, exhausted, sat in the darkened living room and admired the tree before going up to bed themselves.

The rooms upstairs were chilly, and Jeanne made the rounds, pulling up covers, tucking arms and legs back under the blankets. In the boys' room Tim, as usual, had barely disarranged the bedding before falling asleep while Joey's bed, also as usual, looked as though a tornado had blown through. Joey muttered something, moving restlessly, and Jeanne bent to kiss his cheek and say softly, "It's okay, Joey. Nighty-night."

When she joined Hank in their bedroom, he seemed to know how truly tired she was. Once under the covers, he hugged her, kissed her good-night and then cuddled her back against his chest, spoon-fashion.

As she drifted off to sleep, Jeanne's Pollyanna half thought, *See, it isn't just sex.* And her cynical half replied, *No, it isn't just sex—it's a very cold bedroom.*

Twelve

Jeanne rubbed the fogged window of the Blazer with her jacket sleeve, clearing a view of the road. The defroster was on full force, but it couldn't keep up with the breaths of three chattering children. The kids were getting bored waiting for Lisa's bus, but it couldn't be helped.

Jeanne had sensed almost from that first morning when she helped Lisa get ready for school that, although she tried to hide it, the child was edgy about the bus trip home. When, much later, Jeanne mentioned it to Hank, he told her about the time he and Ben were out in the fields longer than expected, and by the time Nora realized she'd better pile the kids in the old Buick and go down the lane, Lisa's bus had already dropped her off and she was walking home alone.

"But she didn't raise a fuss," Hank had said. "She was just really quiet and kind of pinched-face about it."

"Well, it evidently frightened her," Jeanne had responded at the time, "so I'll just be sure to always be there on time, and she'll finally forget to worry about it." So now, no matter if she was wrist-deep in cookie dough or two inches from the end of a seam, when it was time to meet Lisa's bus, she gathered up the kids and hopped into the Blazer.

At last, Lisa's bus arrived. Climbing into the Blazer, Lisa exclaimed before the door closed behind her, "Oh, boy! Christmas vacation!" Then, peering suspiciously at the three children on the back seat, "Did you guys do fun stuff today while I was gone?"

Jeanne answered for them. "Gosh, no! They cleaned the hearths, and beat the rugs and scrubbed the toilets and chopped firewood and..."

"Okay, you're kidding! Daddy doesn't let us use the ax!"

"Oh, all right, I'm kidding," Jeanne confessed. "We made cookies, but I saved some of the dough so you could make some, too." Missing out on the Christmas preparations that took place while she was at school upset Lisa terribly.

"Good. I'm glad you saved some dough for me." Then, in her six-year-old fashion, she was off in another direction. "Don't look in my lunch box. There's a secret there. I'll carry it in the house so you won't see it. The buses came before we even finished eating lunch today." Then she darted back to the original subject—making cookies. "Can I make cookies as soon as we get home?"

Jeanne pulled up by the back door. "Yup. The kids haven't had naps yet, so while they sleep you can make your cookies and I'll finish some sewing." She unlocked the rear of the vehicle and the two boys scrambled out, followed more slowly by a sleepy Emily.

"In the sewing room?" Lisa asked, her voice disappointed.

"No, it's hand-sewing, so I can bring it into the kitchen."

"Good. It wouldn't be much fun by myself."

Tim suddenly got the gist of the conversation. "I'm not sleepy," he said quickly, "not even a little bit!"

"Me, too!" echoed Joey.

Emily clamped off a yawn to add her own, "Me, too."

"Well, that's too bad," Jeanne said sympathetically, "because that means you'll miss the popcorn and movies tonight. If you don't take a nap you can't stay up late."

Tim's small freckled face grew serious as he tried to calculate how he could avoid a nap and still stay up late. "What movies?" he finally asked.

"All those Christmas specials that came on school nights right after Thanksgiving, usually past your bedtime," Jeanne replied. "Daddy taped them all, and tonight we're going to have popcorn and watch as many as we want to—'Rudolph,' 'Frosty,' 'The Night Before Christmas,' and the Walt Disney Christmas special, and—"

"I guess I'll take a nap," Tim decided, and was echoed by his two loyal followers.

"Good choice!" Jeanne complimented him. "Off with the boots and coats, kids." Within thirty minutes the three younger children were down for naps.

Lisa was finishing her leftover lunch. "When is Grandma coming up? I forgot."

"Either tomorrow or Sunday, Christmas Eve," Jeanne replied, "if the weather stays good."

"Well, I hope she can come," Lisa said after a last bite of cheese sandwich. "She would be sad to be alone at Christmas."

"Very sad," Jeanne agreed, "but if the weather stays like it is now, one of us will be able to drive down and bring her back." She looked out the kitchen window doubtfully. The sky had been threatening snow all week, but maybe it would hold off for a little while longer.

The day brightened for her as she saw Hank coming in from the machine shed by the barn. He was walking much, much better these days—still a limp, but not nearly as severe as it had been. He only used a crutch on stairs or when he was extremely tired.

"Here comes your dad, Lisa. Why don't you get him a couple of those one-armed gingerbread men to go with his coffee? Joey and Emily had trouble getting their cookies into the oven without broken arms or legs, but they'll taste just as good."

By the time Hank had washed up and sat down at the kitchen table, Jeanne was able to cover her little rush of emotion by doing a good imitation of a sturdy, practical farm wife. "How's them thar oxen doin', Pa?"

"Purty good, purty good," Hank replied between swallows of gingerbread man. "Ole Belle's kinder stove up in her off hind leg, but Bessie's pullin' hard enough to make up fer it."

Lisa stared at her father. "You're being silly again," she said finally, reaching for the raisins to button up her gingerbread men's coats. "I thought grown-ups weren't supposed to be silly."

Hank winked at Jeanne. Jeanne grinned back, picked up her notepad and began listing the items that weren't life or death, but would certainly come in handy if someone made a trip to town to pick up Ma.

That evening, after Jeanne had removed all traces of the children's baking cookies from the kitchen, everyone gathered around the big table for a light supper. After baths, as they watched the Christmas specials and ate popcorn, the wind came up and began to sigh around the eaves with a lonely, mournful sound. By bedtime the sighs had grown to shrieks, and a pervading cold was creeping across the floors of the old rooms.

As Hank pulled Jeanne across the cold sheets into the warm haven of his arms, she thought for a moment that now she knew why so many of the country wives of older generations greeted each spring pregnant.

Thirteen

Jeanne had fallen asleep in Hank's arms and after what felt like only a few minutes was awakened by noise from downstairs, loud enough to be heard over the howling wind. Hank's side of the bed was empty and very cold. Getting up and jamming her arms into the sleeves of her robe, she hurried down to see Hank limping in with an armful of wood.

"It's wicked out there, a regular blizzard," he said, dumping the wood by the stove. "You'd best keep a fire going all day—that oil guzzler down in the cellar won't keep up with this cold." He stood rubbing his hands together over the warmth of the wood range. "Ben and I are riding up to the high pasture. Got a few early-bred heifers ready to calve mixed in with the rest of the herd up there. Should've brought them down earlier, but this damned leg slowed us down. We can't afford to lose 'em." He headed out for more wood.

"What do I send with you?" Jeanne called after him. "Will you be back for lunch?"

Hank turned at the door. "Just whatever you can throw together in a hurry," he answered, "and no, we won't be back for lunch. We've got an old log shack up there, what's left of a cabin—more like a three-sided lean-to. We'll try to get the heifers in there out of the weather.''

Jeanne sliced ham into an iron skillet and while it sizzled on low heat she ran up and dressed in jeans and flannel shirt. By the time Hank had stacked several armloads of wood on the porch, scrambled eggs were firming in the pan and she was putting thick slabs of ham and cheese between pieces of bread.

Hank came in from the back porch with two dusty kerosene lanterns. ''I'll put these in the pantry,'' he said, ''and if the electricity goes, set one in the kitchen window and one in the side living-room window so we can see them coming in.'' He filled his plate and slid into a chair at the table. ''I didn't intend to wake you up. It's a long time till morning yet, and you were sleeping so nicely.''

''Which must mean I wasn't drooling on the pillow or sleeping with my mouth open,'' Jeanne commented dryly. ''Your intentions were okay, but I would have been really ticked off if I'd woken up to find you'd ridden off into a blizzard!''

Just then Ben came in the back door, accompanied by a gust of cold air and blowing snow. Hank motioned him to the table. ''Pull up a chair, Ben. My wife cooked enough for an army!''

Ben sniffed the warm aroma of fried ham and didn't argue. ''Lemme go tell Nora not to bother. Keep it hot!'' he called over his shoulder as he left for his bungalow.

Hank shook a dollup of catsup on his eggs. ''Could you put together some supplies in case we get stuck up there?'' he said casually.

Jeanne stared at him. ''Stuck up there? For . . . for how long?''

Hank took a big swig of coffee. "Oh, enough for a couple days, just to be safe." Seeing her widened eyes, he quickly added, "Probably won't happen, but best to be ready. Just grab stuff we could heat over a campfire. There's an old coffeepot and iron skillet in the lean-to. The stuff needs to fit in the saddlebags—bacon, coffee, bread, canned hash and chili, all that kind of thing."

The two men ate quickly, then zipped themselves into their heavy down parkas and gloves. Ben went out, and Hank pulled Jeanne into his arms for a hard, quick kiss. Then he stepped from the warm kitchen into the blowing snow on the porch. "Candles and kerosene lamps are in the pantry, remember," he called over his shoulder. "Take care!"

Take care, Jeanne thought bleakly. "You take care!" she shouted from the doorway, but her voice was lost in the shrieking wind. She went upstairs to make sure the children were sleeping warmly, and found them cuddled snugly together under their blankets and patchwork quilts. She thought about going back to bed, but she was too edgy for sleep, so she turned on the electric heater in the sewing room and finished up the doll clothes for Lisa and Emily.

Fourteen

Although Jeanne hadn't thought it possible, the storm increased in fury. As night finally became morning, daylight only added to her anxiety, when she realized that visibility was less than two feet. Although she could see nothing beyond the wall of blowing snow, her eyes went often to the kitchen window facing the high pasture, where she knew Hank was headed.

It felt like afternoon when the kids finally came downstairs, but the clock said it was only twenty after eight. Blown snow was plastered against the windows, and the combination of howling wind and white windows unnerved the kids, Jeanne could tell. The two younger children looked ready to cry, and Jeanne was especially touched by Tim's and Lisa's attempts to appear unaffected.

"How about teddy-bear pancakes for breakfast?" she asked, hoping to take their minds off the storm.

"Teddy-bear pancakes?" Tim said, ever the cautious one. "I never had them before. Have you, Lisa?"

"No," his sister answered, "but I bet they're good." As Jeanne had hoped, they all gathered around with fears temporarily forgotten as she ladled circles of batter for the bear's head and ears, and gave him chocolate chips for eyes and nose.

The electricity went off just as the ears of the last teddy bear were being eaten. The noise of the storm had been somewhat muted by the distant murmur of television cartoons from the living room and soft carols from the radio on the kitchen counter. In their absence, the sounds of the storm seemed even more menacing than before. "I wish Daddy was here," Lisa said in a small voice.

Oh, honey, so do I! thought Jeanne. Aloud she said, "Come help me get the candles and lamps, kids."

The sound of someone at the back door brought Jeanne a momentary rush of relief, but it was only Nora. She came in, snow crusting her jacket and her stocking cap, which was pulled down over her ears. "I thought you might be afraid," she said, rubbing her hands over the heat of the wood range, "and I wanted to be sure you didn't go outside without using the rope."

"The rope?" Jeanne asked. "What rope?"

"The rope hanging by the back door," Nora answered. "A person could get turned around out there, lose their sense of direction and not be able to get back to the house. There's a rope by your back door and ours, and one out at the barn, too."

Jeanne shivered as she hurried to the sink to fill the coffeepot. No water came from the faucet. "The pump works on electricity," Nora said calmly, turning to get a large soup kettle from the pantry. "You'll have to start a pan of snow melting." Opening the back door, Jeanne saw they wouldn't have to leave the safety of the porch to scoop up snow; the wind had drifted it against the back steps and onto the wooden flooring.

"Nora, what about the men?" Jeanne shouted above the roar of the storm.

Nora closed the door behind them before she answered. "They're holed up in the lean-to with a fire going," she reassured the younger woman. "They know the weather, and the horses know how to get home." But to Jeanne, the words seemed to lack conviction.

Nora stayed only long enough to see that Jeanne and the children were able to manage alone, then pulled on her jacket, stocking cap and boots again. Jeanne urged her to stay, but the older woman shook her head.

"Got to keep the fire going, or we'll have frozen pipes," she explained, "and I turned off the lantern when I left—never safe to leave candles or lamps burning when you're not around to tend 'em." She pulled on her mittens and stopped with her hand on the doorknob. "I've got to get back and light it. They'd see our window sooner than they'd see yours on the way back. It's closer."

The house was cooling rapidly, and Jeanne realized the furnace wasn't working. *Well, of course, you idiot. Even an oil furnace would have an electric motor.* She hurried to add wood to the fire that was almost out in the living-room fireplace.

The day wore on slowly, a continuous round of stoking fires while trying to proceed with the usual tasks of the day so the children wouldn't be frightened. Darkness came early, a gradual dimming of the luminescent whiteness at the windows, and Jeanne had to face the fact that she and the children would probably spend the night alone. She knew the stack of wood on the porch would never last the night, so, instructing the children that Lisa was in charge and they were not to touch the candles or lamps, she pulled on Hank's old work coat and boots, and stepped quickly out the back door.

The wind hit her like a physical blow, and she grabbed in panic for the rope tied to a large hook by the door. It trailed off into the snow, and she pulled steadily until the ice-crusted end was in her hands, then after a moment of indecision, tied it around her waist. With a desperation fueled by wind and fear, she plunged in the direction of the woodshed, filled her arms with logs and plodded back to dump them on the porch. She made trip after trip until she was sure there was enough to last the night, then untied the rope and gratefully stumbled into the warmth of the kitchen.

For a few moments she could do nothing but beat her numb, mittened hands together, but finally stinging needles of pain told her that circulation was returning.

Jeanne heated soup on the wood range for their supper, and by eight o'clock the children were all settled on the living-room floor. Jeanne had carried quilts and blankets from their beds; without the furnace the upstairs was far too cold. She closed off the living room to hold the heat in, hoping that enough warmth from the kitchen stove would creep up the stairs to keep the bathroom pipes from freezing. She sat with the children, reading the old familiar Christmas stories and making up new ones till they finally fell asleep.

Then she brought her paperback mystery from the bedroom, made herself coffee on the wood range and sat with it at the kitchen table. She didn't feel sleepy yet, but didn't want to take a chance on nodding off in the warm comfort of the living-room couch. She had to stay awake, she told herself, to keep the fires stoked. And most importantly, in the kitchen she would be more likely to hear outside noises. What if Hank managed to get close enough that a call for help could be heard over the storm, she thought, and she was sleeping and didn't hear him?

Each time her eyelids began to droop, Jeanne roused herself and made a tour of the house—stoked the fires, pulled the quilts up around the shoulders of the sleeping children—then returned to the kitchen. In the lonely small hours of the morning she made more coffee and sat with it, the paperback facedown on the table. Added to the shrieking of the wind were the small, comfortable inside noises—the fire snapping, the quiet hiss of bubbles rising to the surface of the pot on the stove, the old house creaking as it cooled, the ticking of the grandfather clock in the living room. She hurried in to wind it as she had seen Hank do, relieved that it hadn't started to lose time yet. Then she returned to the kitchen and sat warming her shaking fingers around her coffee cup.

Why am I being so silly? she asked herself. Hank and Ben know what they're doing. They're holed up in that shack, perfectly safe. They're dressed warmly and have food and shelter.

Then the frightened child deep inside took over. What if they weren't able to make it to the shack? What if they couldn't find it and they're riding in circles out there in the blizzard? What if the horse stepped in a hole and broke a leg?

She saw a bleak future without Hank stretching out before her. Oh, yes, they had started all the proper legal steps to protect her and the children if something should happen to Hank. But what would *she* do without him? They'd been so calm and sensible in arranging their marriage, and then somewhere along the way she had fallen in love. Pushing aside the coffee cup, she rested her face on her folded arms and cried quietly.

A small hand stroked her hair, and Lisa pleaded, "Don't be scared. It's only the wind."

Jeanne wiped her face with a flannel-clad forearm. "I know. I guess I'm just...just a sissy. What are you doing up? Did you get cold?"

"No, I think I got too hot. Em was squinched up on one side of me and Joey on the other side. I'm all sweaty—feel my neck." Then, with one of her usual conversational swings, she asked, "What time is it?"

Jeanne looked at her watch. "It's almost three in the morning—Christmas Eve morning."

"I guess Grandma won't be coming, will she?"

"Nope. And we won't be going anyplace, either."

Lisa sighed. "Well, I just want Daddy to get back, that's all. Only us is really all we need to have Christmas."

"You're right," Jeanne agreed, "only us." She shivered. "I'm glad you're awake. I need to go for more wood, and you can be in charge of the lamps."

Fifteen

Plunging through the snow with the rope around her waist, it seemed to Jeanne that the wind was a little less fierce than it had been on her previous trip. In a momentary lull she held her breath while she listened for shouts or the sound of horses. Then the wind renewed its fury, as though trying to make up for the few seconds lost.

Back inside, Jeanne had cocoa with Lisa and then tucked the little girl back under her quilts and blankets. "Stay here till I go to sleep, okay?" Lisa asked.

"Sure," Jeanne answered, sinking gratefully onto the soft couch for just a few minutes.

She woke with a start, uncertain which had awakened her, the cold or the silence. The wind had stopped. She dashed to the kitchen and laid kindling over the embers in the big iron stove, then blew the fire to life. Back in the living room, the children awakened as she stirred the coals in the fireplace. "Stay under the covers till it gets a little warmer," she instructed.

"Is Daddy home yet?" Tim asked.

"No, honey, not yet, but I bet he'll be here soon. The storm is over."

"Is it Christmas yet?" Emily's voice was still sleepy.

Jeanne looked at the grandfather clock. "It's Christmas Eve morning. As soon as it warms up a bit, we're going to put away these blankets and get dressed, and then we're going to make a big pot of vegetable soup to thaw out your daddy when he comes home. Then we're going to finish getting ready for Christmas."

She kept them busy, for her own comfort, as well as theirs. The turkey was thawing in the nonfunctioning refrigerator, and the children crumbled bread for stuffing and pinged frozen cranberries into the pan. They crimped piecrust around the edges and carried cans and jars from the pantry.

Nora came over to check on them midmorning. She accepted a cup of tea from Jeanne and looked around the busy kitchen with a grin. "Well, shoot, I don't have to worry about you folks. You're managing just fine!"

After the brief visit, Jeanne followed Nora to the door where the kids wouldn't hear. "Shouldn't the men be home by now, Nora?" she asked.

Nora gazed out at the white expanse. "No need to worry yet," she said quietly. "The horses'll have to break a trail all the way. It'll be a long trip." She pulled the stocking cap down over her ears. "I'm hopin' they'll get here by dark." She set off for her own house, carefully stepping in the holes she'd made on her trip over.

The sun came out briefly during the day and, combined with the heat from inside, melted the snow that had stuck to the windows. "Look!" Tim cried, "the fences are covered!" Jeanne looked out at the white world with dismay. How could horses struggle home through snow so deep? No fences to guide them, landmarks covered with snow... She turned away from the window.

As the early dusk began to fall, Jeanne refilled the kerosene lamps and set them in the windows. What was she to do? She'd been brave for the children, but her stock of courage was just about used up. Another cold, lonely night to get through, and then it would be Christmas—and no Hank. At what point, she wondered, do Nora or I try to go for help? She lifted the chimney of the lamp and struck a match. As she carefully replaced the glass she heard noise on the back porch. Afraid to get her hopes up this time, she stood motionless until the door swung open.

Hank stumbled in.

She was across the kitchen in a few bounds, in his arms, patting his cold face with her fingertips to prove that he was really, truly there, crying, laughing and talking all at once. "You scared me to death!" she gasped, tears streaking her cheeks. "Don't you ever do that again! Are you all right? How's your ankle? Are you—"

Hank silenced her with his lips. When the long kiss ended, Jeanne rested her head against his chest, the strong thud of his heart comforting her. The four children clamored around them, filling the air with questions.

From city-kid Emily: "Did you save the cow babies, Daddy?"

From Lisa, Tim and Joey: "Did you sleep in the shed? Did the horses drink snow?

From all of them, a chorus of "Daddy, Daddy, tomorrow's Christmas!"

I don't care who says what first anymore, Jeanne thought. To hell with pride. "Oh, Hank, I—"

He interrupted her. "Jeanne, Jeanne—" the words were caresses "—I hadn't told you how much I love you. I kept thinking, what if something happens and I never get to tell her I love her?" His chilled fingers awkwardly brushed the tears from her cheeks and then framed her face as he kissed her again, a kiss so deep she felt herself falling into it.

"Oh," she whispered, "oh, I love you, too—so much!"

At that moment, Jeanne realized she'd become a princess, after all.

My Valentine 1994

Celebrate the most romantic day of the year with
MY VALENTINE 1994
a collection of original stories, written by
four of Harlequin's most popular authors...

MARGOT DALTON
MURIEL JENSEN
MARISA CARROLL
KAREN YOUNG

Available in February, wherever
Harlequin Books are sold.

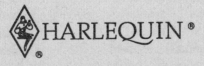

HARLEQUIN ®

VAL94

NEW YORK TIMES Bestselling Author

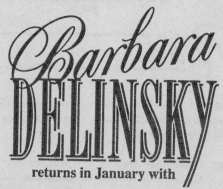

Barbara DELINSKY

returns in January with

THE REAL THING

Stranded on an island off the coast of Maine,
Deirdre Joyce and Neil Hersey got the
solitude they so desperately craved—
but they also got each other, something they
hadn't expected. Nor had they expected
to be consumed by a desire so powerful
that the idea of living alone again was
unimaginable. A marrige of "convenience"
made sense—or did it?   B0B7

 HARLEQUIN®

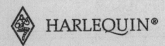